live and let pie

Twin Berry Bakery - 4

wendy meadows

Majestic Owl Publishing LLC
P.O. Box 997
Newport, NH 03773

chapter one

Rhonda watched Zach lift a heavy bale of hay. "Working hard?" she asked through chattering teeth. A bitter cold wind was whispering in around a dreary gray morning scented with snow.

Zach spotted Rhonda standing in the barn door holding a cup of coffee. The early morning light made her face glow with a beauty that Zach couldn't putinto words. He liked Rhonda—a lot—but wasn't prepared to confess his feelings.

"Billy wanted this hay stacked," he said. He tossed the bale of hay he was holding down onto a neatly stacked row and then slapped at the work gloves covering his hands. "Now that the Pumpkin Festival is over, there isn't really much for me to do. Billy finds a few odds and ends to keep me busy."

"I don't think it's that there's no work," Rhonda pointed out, feeling grateful that she had tossed fashion to the side and worn a warm gray and white coat to Billy's farm. "Billy said we're going to have a terrible winter this year. This freezing weather arrived overnight."

Zach knew Rhonda was right. All the work Billy had planned for Zach to accomplish had been hampered by days of freezing rain and icy winds. Yet, Billy, staying good to his word, kept finding little jobs for Zach to do instead of handing him a pink slip. "Billy is paying me good money to stack hay. I feel like I'm cheating the man."

Rhonda took a sip of her coffee and studied Zach. The poor man was wearing only a thin green windbreaker over a pair of worn jeans. His head was covered with the usual ball cap he always wore, hiding a handsome face that Rhonda was very fond of. "Rita and I came to say goodbye," she explained. "Rita will be here in a minute."

"Goodbye?" Zach asked, confused. "Where are you two girls going to?"

"Mayfield, Vermont," Rhonda told Zach, feeling a gust of icy wind push her further into the shadowy barn. The scents of heavy hay, cold dirt, and cows greeted her nose. Far above her head, nestled in the haylofts, she heard pigeons cooing. "A friend of Rita's has invited us up to her lake cabin for a week."

Zach grabbed another bale of hay. "Sounds like fun."

"Not really," Rhonda confessed. "Paula Capperson isn't exactly the type of woman that goes well with my personality."

"Oh?" Zach tossed the bale of hay onto one of the neatly stacked rows resting in front of him.

Rhonda sipped at her coffee. "Yeah," she said. "Zach, you know by now that I like to cut up, laugh, and joke around."

"Sure." Zach nodded. Deep down Zach was not only falling in love with Rhonda's beauty but also her sense of humor. He admired how the woman could joke around even when times were tough. "There's nothing wrong with having a sense of humor."

"Tell Paula Capperson that," Rhonda complained. "Paula is the type of woman that would make a piece of square wood seem fascinating in comparison. She's...so anal. Everything—everyone—has to be in a precise order." Rhonda rolled her eyes. "The topic of which type of weeds to pull from your flower bed makes good dinner talk for the woman."

"Then why go?" Zach asked, his brow furrowed.

"Two words: my sister," Rhonda groaned. "Rita is blackmailing me."

Zach fought back a grin. He liked how Rhonda and Rita got after each other sometimes. "Oh?"

Rhonda sipped more coffee. "Either I go or she tells our parents I was nearly killed falling out of the back of a truck," she told Zach in a miserable voice. "If my darling sister was to carry out such a heinous act, my parents would scream at me until my ears fell off. And with Thanksgiving being so close…oh, Rita is good. Good, I tell you."

Zach grabbed a third bale of hay. "Yeah, I guess she is a little tricky. You can sue her. I'll represent you. The cows in this barn can be the jurors and Billy can be the judge. You'd win for sure."

"Funny." Rhonda stuck her tongue out at him. Zach didn't see. "Well, anyway, I thought I'd say goodbye."

Zach nodded. "I'll see you in a week."

"A week…seven days…one hundred and sixty-eight hours…ten thousand and eighty minutes…" Rhonda nearly sobbed. "Six hundred four thousand and eight hundred seconds…"

"Beginning when you arrive," Zach teased Rhonda. "You're leaving out the travel time."

"Not funny, you." Rhonda gave him a mock glare. "Paula Capperson is serious business. That woman can zap the fun out of Bugs Bunny."

"I kinda liked Foghorn Leghorn better."

Rhonda narrowed her eyes. "Don't mess with the Bunny," she warned.

Zach threw his hands up in the air and backed off. "Okay…okay," he said. "This unemployed lawyer won't insult Bugs Bunny."

Rhonda quickly reminded herself that Zach was still working through his own troubles and knocked off the joking. "I guess things haven't been easy for you, huh?" she asked.

Zach shrugged. "Most of my money goes to the government," he explained. "My ex-wife ran up a lot of bills she chained to my wrists. I either pay or risk going to jail." Zach looked around the barn. "I'm grateful to Billy. He's really helping me keep my head above water."

"Billy is a good man," Rhonda said and then, on very careful legs, asked: "Zach, the bakery did exceptionally well this season…better than Rita and I could have ever dreamed." Rhonda took a sip of coffee. "Erma, of course, is the real reason the bakery did so well. Anyway…um…we have some extra money, and if you need—"

"I'm okay," Zach promised Rhonda, cutting her off at the pass. "Billy lets me sleep in the guest room and feeds me three square meals a day. He pays me more than I really earn, too. Plus," Zach added, "Jose and his family have basically adopted me. Jose's mother brings me food and is always shoving a few dollars into my pocket. The poor woman thinks I'm destitute." Zach smiled at the thought of Jose's mother. "I'm growing very fond of the woman."

"I love Jose's mother," Rhonda agreed. "Sweetest woman in the world. And she sure keeps Billy in his place."

Zach nodded. "Sweet as apple pie," he said and then went back to his work. "Well…have a good trip, okay? I better get this hay stacked. Billy wants me to help Jose work on a conveyer belt later. I know Jose doesn't need the help, but if it makes Billy happy."

"It sure does," Billy said in his southern farmer's voice. "Jose is going to show you how to troubleshoot them there conveyer belts and tractors to boot."

Zach saw Billy step up beside Rhonda wearing a thick

brown pair of overalls and his ball cap. "Jose does a good job at those chores, Billy."

"Why, sure he does." Billy nodded as Rhonda joined him. "But a man who ain't willing to learn ain't worth much. Jose can teach you new skills that will sure come in handy next year when the Pumpkin Festival swings back through." Billy motioned around the barn. "Man can only do so much in a barn. I've got to get you oiled and ready for next year, Zach."

"I...wasn't aware you would keep me on that long," Zach confessed.

"Why sure," Billy said in an easy voice. "I intend to keep you on the farm until you grow old and tired. That is, if you don't go running off on me. I mean, a man might get the need to move on later on. But just know this here farm will always have a place for you." Billy looked at Rita, who had just arrived. Rita was smiling at him. "What?" he asked.

"You're very sweet." Rita quickly kissed Billy's cheek. Billy turned redder than a summer tomato. "Well, I guess we better get on the road. Ready, Sis?"

Rhonda looked at Rita, who was wearing a black leather jacket that didn't seem warm. She stalled and let her sister... chill out. "Oh, not yet," she said, listening to the icy winds rip through the barn. Rita tucked at the leather jacket and eased closer to Billy. "Zach and I aren't through talking yet."

Rita knew what her sister was up to. Rhonda had warned her to wear a warm coat, but Rita had chosen the leather jacket because she wanted to look fashionable for Billy. But Billy—being his normal sensible self—had asked her why she was wearing a rain jacket instead of a warm coat. "Can you make your goodbye sooner than later?" she asked, feeling the winds grab at her free-flowing hair. Rhonda, the smarty pants, had a warm pink ski cap covering her hair.

"Oh, what's the rush?" Rhonda took a sip of her hot coffee. "Coffee is good," she said and patted the coffee cup with a pair of gloved hands. Rita wasn't even wearing gloves.

For a woman who thrived on being practical, she was dressed very impractically. The only practical decision Rita had made today was to wear a long, warm, blue dress.

Rita glared at her twin sister. "Rhonda, we really need to get on the road. We have to be at the airport in less than three hours," she stated through teeth beginning to chatter.

Billy looked at Rita. "Why, you're turning blue," he exclaimed and shook his head. "Can't see why you wore that there rain jacket instead of a warm coat. Sure hope you dress warmer in Vermont."

"Thanks...Billy," Rita said and threw her eyes back at Rhonda. "Say goodbye to Zach."

Rhonda grinned. "Okay, okay," she said and handed Rita her coffee. "Warm your hands and your insides."

Billy shook his head again. "Sometimes you two are mighty hard to figure out," he said and then focused on Zach. "When you're finished stacking the hay, go up into the hayloft and shovel out the loose hay and feed it to the milk cows, okay? I'll be shoveling out the manure."

"Hey, Billy...let me do that. You shovel the hay," Zach pleaded.

"I've been shoveling manure all my life. Ain't nothing to it," he told Zach. "Man can't ignore the little jobs he's used to doing just because he has a friend at his side. No sir."

Rita looked into Billy's sweet eyes. Sure, she was freezing, but Billy's heart was warming her own heart. "I'll call you when we arrive in Vermont, okay, Billy?"

Billy saw Rita staring into his eyes and blushed. Why in the world such a beautiful woman was showing him attention, he sure didn't know. "I reckon that would be a good idea," he said and let out a clumsy smile. "I reckon... well..." Billy leaned forward, kissed Rita on her cheek, and hurried off.

Rhonda looked at Rita and grinned. "He's a real

romantic," she said and waved at Zach. "I'll see you when we get back, okay?"

"You bet." Zach smiled in a way that told Rhonda he was looking forward to seeing her again. Rhonda blushed and hurried out of the barn with Rita.

"Zach's a nice guy," Rita said, making a straight line for her SUV.

Rhonda glanced over her shoulder and saw Zach go back to stacking hay. "Yeah, I guess he is," she admitted.

Rita hurried around Billy's old truck and then dashed into the driver's seat of her SUV. "Get in. I'll get the heat going."

"I wasn't planning on walking," Rhonda called out. She hurried to the passenger's door, climbed inside the SUV, and took her coffee from Rita. "Well," she said, "off we go to see Ms. Square Wood."

Rita snapped on the heat. "Rhonda, Paula is a close friend. And," Rita added in a serious voice, "she was a good cop."

"Paula Capperson moved to Vermont and took a desk job," Rhonda argued as the front vents began throwing warm air into her face. "She spent a lot less time patrolling there than the streets in Atlanta."

"Well...maybe so, but she proved herself during that time."

"She ran down a sixty-eight-year-old shoplifter who stole his ex-wife's purse out of spite," Rhonda told Rita and rolled her eyes. "The guy had one leg that was shorter than the other."

Rita felt her cheeks turn red. "What do you have against Paula?" she demanded. "Paula was always very friendly toward you."

"For starters," Rhonda fired back, "she has absolutely no sense of humor."

"Oh, here we go," Rita complained.

"I'm serious," Rhonda fussed. "Paula Capperson would

think a clown...farting in his sleep...had a serious medical condition."

"Do you have to be so...crude?" Rita asked. "Can we keep our words ladylike?"

Rhonda rolled her eyes. "Rita, your so-called dear friend is about as interesting as a stink bug waddling through a mud puddle."

Rita threw her eyes at Rhonda. "Why...I'm tempted to not even bring you along."

"Please don't," Rhonda begged.

"I've already paid for your plane ticket," Rita snapped.

Billy stuck his head out of the barn with Zach, spotted Rita and Rhonda going at each other, and shook his head. "They'll sit there and chew at one another for an hour. I've seen them do it before," he told Zach. "Best if we just go back to our chores and let them be."

"Yeah...I guess we better," Zach agreed and walked back into the barn with Billy.

"Oh, you're impossible sometimes," Rhonda griped at Rita. "First you blackmail me into going, and now you're—"

"I did not blackmail you. I simply...made you an offer you could not refuse," Rita informed Rhonda, feeling like a silly schoolgirl. "Okay...okay...maybe I did twist your arm... a little."

"A lot," Rhonda corrected her sister.

"Okay, I admit that I'm forcing you to take this trip with me. That's only because..." Rita paused.

"Because what?" Rhonda asked warily. She looked into her sister's eyes. "Rita, what's going on?"

Rita drew in a deep breath. "Paula...is getting married, Rhonda. We're...attending a wedding...not staying at a lakeside cabin."

"What?" Rhonda exclaimed. "Rita...how could you?"

"I know you hate weddings, I had to trick you because...I

didn't want to go alone," Rita claimed in a miserable voice. "Please don't be upset with me."

Rhonda looked down at her coffee with upset eyes. "Get us to the airport," she said through gritted teeth. "The sooner we get this nightmare over with, the better."

Rita threw the SUV into reverse and got moving. "We'll have fun," she promised. "You'll see. The wedding will be...fun."

Rhonda closed her eyes and began taking deep breaths. "Just remind yourself the woman is your sister...just remind yourself the woman is your sister...just remind yourself the woman is your sister."

Billy saw Rita drive away. "Yep," he said, knowing the truth, and went to shoveling manure.

Paula Capperson was a very ugly woman. She reminded Rhonda of her old third grade teacher, Mrs. Elkworth. Mrs. Elkworth had the longest, sharpest nose Rhonda had ever seen. The nose matched an ugly, cruel face consumed with tiny eyes filled with sour hatred.

"Rita, Rhonda, how nice of you to make the trip," Paula Capperson said in a monotone voice that matched her dull face. She took Rita's hand and gave it a soft squeeze. "How was your flight?"

"Oh, fine," Rita said and tossed a warning look at Rhonda. She saw Rhonda staring at Paula's hair. The poor woman was wearing what appeared to be some type of perm that didn't sit well with hair that had been recently dyed black.

"Uh...yeah, fine," Rhonda added. "The drive up to this town was...snowy."

Paula studied Rita's and Rhonda's matching gray and blue coats. The two sisters were identical, which was a bit annoying. The only difference Paula could make between the two sisters was the dresses they were wearing. A warm, lightly colored blue dress was sticking out from under Rita's coat. Rhonda was wearing a dark green dress. "I suppose you might need to change your coats at a later time," she pointed out. "Otherwise, no one will know who's who."

Rhonda glanced around the fancy foyer she was standing in. The foyer smelled of snobby talk. "Uh...yeah," she said and tossed her eyes down at the brown boots she was wearing. Paula had made sure she had stomped every bit of snow off the boots before stepping into the foyer. "Rita and I both saw these coats on sale at the same time. Same thing with our boots."

Rita quickly helped her sister. "I'll go into town and buy another coat," she assured Paula.

"I would appreciate that," Paula told Rita and offered a pale smile. "Now, I have coffee prepared in the kitchen along with some bran muffins. Shall we?"

"Uh...sure." Rita smiled.

Paula nodded, checked the bland pinkish-colored dress she had chosen to wear for the day, and left the foyer.

"Shoot me," Rhonda begged.

"Stop it," Rita whispered.

Rhonda grimaced and followed her sister past a wooden stairwell holding glossy steps. "I feel like I'm in a museum," she murmured.

Rita shot Rhonda a hard eye as she followed Paula down a fancy hallway lined with paintings and antique furnishings that, well, did look as if they had come from a museum. The hallway ended at a medium-sized kitchen that was way too fancy to cook in.

"Oh, what a lovely kitchen," Rita told Paula.

Rhonda stepped up beside Rita and walked her eyes around the kitchen. She spotted a glossy hardwood floor, glossy wooden cabinets that must have cost a small fortune, and a wooden island stove and a round kitchen table sitting next to a set of double glass doors covered with thick blue drapes. The kitchen was in immaculate order. "Fancy."

Rita elbowed Rhonda when Paula's back was turned. "The coffee smells great."

"I order my coffee from Switzerland," Paula explained in a snooty voice. She strolled over to a silver coffee tray holding fancy little white coffee cups decorated with tiny little red birds wearing tiny little bows. "I drink my coffee black. I do, however, have milk in the refrigerator if you prefer."

"No...no, we like our coffee black, too," Rita said as she quickly soaked in the kitchen. "It's good to see you again, Paula. We haven't seen you in—"

"Years," Paula told Rita in her bland voice. "Yes, I know."

"I was very surprised when you contacted me," Rita said.

"You were?" Rhonda whispered.

Rita elbowed her sister again. "Rhonda and I are very honored to be guests at your wedding."

"We are?" Rhonda asked.

Rita stomped on Rhonda's foot. "A snowy wedding is... very romantic," she said and gave Rhonda a "don't-say-a-word" face.

"Yes, I suppose," Paula said as she worked on filling the cups with expensive coffee.

"You...haven't really told me much about the man you're going to marry," Rita said. She decided to take a seat at the kitchen table. Paula watched Rita sit down and then shook her head. Rita frowned. "What? Did I do something wrong?"

"That's my seat," Paula explained.

"Oh...sorry." Rita quickly changed seats, ignoring Rhonda's "are you serious?" expression. "Better?" Paula nodded yes and went back to the coffee. Rhonda rolled her eyes and joined her sister at the table. "So...who's the lucky man?" Rita asked.

"His name is Oscar Frost," Paula told Rita. Rhonda

quickly turned her head and bit on her lip. Rita kicked her foot. "Oscar is an author."

"Oh," Rita said, desperately trying to show interest, "has he written anything I might have read?"

Paula grew silent for a second. "I don't think so," she finally spoke. "Oscar is...still working on his first novel."

"Oh...I see," Rita said and looked at Rhonda, who was trying not to pop a gut. "Stop," she whispered.

"Oscar Frost..." Rhonda giggled under her breath. "Oh boy..."

Paula turned away from the kitchen counter and carried the coffee over to the kitchen table and set it down. "Oscar is a very wealthy man," she continued and carefully handed Rita and Rhonda each a cup of coffee. "He comes from a very respected bloodline."

Rita nodded. "That's nice."

"Indeed," Paula agreed. "Oscar's parents were both bankers in New York. Very distinguished."

Rhonda took her coffee and decided to change the subject. "Paula, forgive me for asking, but you never seemed like the type of woman who...wanted to pursue a career in law enforcement. Why did you decide to become a cop?"

Rita moaned. "Paula, I'm so sorry—"

"No, no, Rhonda's question is a very practical one," Paula said as she took her seat. "Rhonda, to answer your question, I must first explain that I had no interest in becoming a cop. You are both aware that I was raised by my grandparents, right?"

"Nope," Rhonda said, and Rita kicked her foot again; it was starting to throb a bit. "Uh...oh, that's right, I remember."

Paula continued. "My grandfather was a retired cop and insisted that I follow in his footsteps. He went through great pains to get me into the police academy. But, oh, how I detested it all." Paula took a sip of her coffee. "Sadly, my grandfather died shortly after I graduated from the academy."

"I'm sorry," Rita said.

"So was I, but not for the reasons you might expect," Paula explained. "I loved my grandfather but resented him for forcing me to live his dream. After he died, the resentment I felt toward him transferred into guilt. It was that guilt that kept me on the force. Then one day I decided it was time to stop feeling guilty. I made up a simple lie about accepting a new position in Vermont and moved away. I went to college and became a teacher."

"Mrs. Elkworth," Rhonda whispered. Rita kicked her foot again, shooting her sister a glare. Rhonda grinned.

"I still teach to this day at a private academy," Paula continued. "I get paid very good money."

"But why lie?" Rita asked. "Paula, you're a grown woman who is fully capable of making decisions for herself."

"I lied, Rita," Paula said, "because I did not want to hurt my grandmother. It was easier to disguise my true intentions rather than allow her to see my grandfather's dream go up, as they say, in smoke. Fortunately, my grandmother passed many years ago without discovering the truth."

Rita took a sip of her coffee. It tasted like mud. "Well...I understand," she told Paula and faked a yawn. "Paula, do forgive me, but it has been a long trip. I believe Rhonda and I will go back to our hotel room and rest for a while."

"You will return for dinner at seven sharp, correct?" Paula asked.

"Of course," Rita promised. She stood up and thanked Paula for the coffee. "Rhonda and I can't wait to meet Oscar Frost."

"We sure can't." Rhonda grinned. Rita shot her a sharp eye.

Paula stood up. "I'll be serving a very simple dinner," she explained.

"Pizza?" Rhonda asked in a hopeful voice.

To Rita's shock, Paula nodded yes. "Really?" Rita asked.

Paula made a dreadful face. "My soon-to-be husband has an awful taste for pizza, I'm afraid. He insisted that I serve pizza tonight along with root beer. Please do not be offended."

"Offended?" Rhonda asked. "Paula, pizza and root beer rocks my socks."

Rita moaned. "What my sister means to say is that pizza and root beer will be fine," she promised, gently patting Paula's hand. "We can see ourselves to the door."

"Of course," Paula said. She watched Rita and Rhonda begin to leave the kitchen and then, against her will, called out: "Wait. Rita?"

"Yes?" Rita asked. She turned around and saw a pained expression cover Paula's face. "Paula, what's wrong?"

Paula slowly sat back down. "Rita…you…and Rhonda… are the only guests who will be attending my wedding," she said in a destroyed voice. "No one else will be there because…I have no other friends…and neither does Oscar."

Rita looked at Rhonda. Rhonda was no longer smiling. "Really?" Rhonda asked. "No friends at all?"

Paula shook her head. "I have always been a very private woman," she explained. "I keep my personal life private from my co-workers. And Oscar…well, he's…different."

"Different?" Rita asked. She eased back over to the kitchen table. "What do you mean by different?"

"Eccentric," Paula explained. "Oscar Frost is a very eccentric person. His personality sometimes has a tendency to put other people off."

Rhonda scratched the back of her head. "Paula, forgive me for being so frank, but you don't seem like the type of woman who would marry Mr. Bubbly."

"I have to agree with my sister," Rita added.

"I would also agree," Paula confirmed. She took a sip of

her coffee. "I met Oscar at the local writers' club. We met every Wednesday night at seven o'clock. Unfortunately, there weren't very many members." Paula set down her coffee. "One Wednesday last year, Oscar and I were the only two members in attendance. We decided to allow the meeting to take place. To my shock, I realized I enjoyed Oscar's company and he enjoyed mine. We agreed to become friends and began holding private meetings in my kitchen." Paula looked down at her hands. "To be perfectly honest, neither Oscar nor I felt very welcome at the writers' club. We did, however, feel very comfortable meeting in my kitchen."

"So you ended up falling in love?" Rhonda asked.

"I'm not sure how to describe it," Paula answered Rhonda. "Oscar isn't the type of man a woman can have a future with. I'm not the type of woman a man can have a future with. Oscar and I decided to marry one another based off the fact that we're both...lonely and in need of companionship."

"Paula, why are you telling us this?" Rita asked in a soft voice. "You have no need to explain yourself to me, or anyone else for that matter."

Paula lifted her eyes. "Rita, I'm confessing the truth because I want you and Rhonda both to understand that I'm not a popular woman and Oscar isn't a popular man. We're social outcasts, you might say. Yes, while I may teach at a private academy, I only do so because the parents of my students desire a teacher who is hard and cold and insists the students do the work. I failed at trying to develop a career in the public school system. Parents complained—often. I was very blessed to receive a teaching position at the private academy I currently teach at." Paula glanced at Rhonda. "Oscar and I are going to get married at the local courthouse. I needed two witnesses. I...had no one else to turn to and...I didn't want a cruel person working at the courthouse acting annoyed because they had to act as a witness. I suppose my pride has stepped in and—"

"Rhonda and I will be proud to stand up for you," Rita assured Paula, patting her hand. "Say no more."

"Yeah…just make sure you order a large cheese pizza for me," Rhonda joked. "And lots and lots of root beer. I usually stay on a diet but tonight we'll throw caution to the wind and get fat." Rhonda thought of Zach. "Well…not too fat."

To Rita's relief, Paula actually smiled a real, authentic smile. "Thank you," she said in a grateful voice. "I realize that I am a very stuffy person who is difficult to know. I don't explain my emotions very well, and my voice is void of life. I wish I could change, but I can't. I'm content with who I am and that makes me happy." Paula stood up. "My students assume I am a very cold person, but I actually do care about their minds. I'm simply the type of woman who is better forgotten. But while I am alive, I do wish to have some form of happiness."

Rita felt her heart break. "Oh, Paula, you're not better off forgotten," she promised. Then an idea struck Rita's mind. "Paula, do you have to get married in the courthouse?"

"Well, I'm a Methodist and Oscar is nondenominational," Paula explained. "It seemed fitting to us to get married there since neither of us attend a local church."

"What are you thinking?" Rhonda asked Rita. "Keep in mind it's snowing outside."

Rita bit down on her lower lip. "We'll have the wedding at the courthouse but have the reception here."

"I…" Paula sighed. "Rita, I just admitted that I lied to you. There are no guests. I was going to lie and tell you that all of my guests had to cancel, leaving only you two. But no. There aren't, and never were, any other guests."

"So we'll have a very small reception." Rita smiled. "Rhonda and I will come over tonight and we'll put up decorations, order a wedding cake, and—"

"No," Paula told Rita in a grateful but stern voice. "I do appreciate your offer, Rita, but a simple ceremony is all Oscar and I want and—" Before Paula could finish her sentence, the kitchen window shattered. Paula screamed.

"Down!" Rita yelled and hit the floor. Rhonda joined her. Rita threw her eyes around and spotted a brick wrapped with a note. "Look there," she told Rhonda. Rhonda quickly grabbed the brick and yanked the note off. "What does it say?"

"'Leave town or die,'" Rhonda read aloud. She looked at Paula. "Looks like you may not have many friends, but you sure have an enemy."

Paula stared at Rita and Rhonda with unblinking eyes. She didn't say a word. Outside in the snow, a shadowy figure eased behind a set of snowy trees and vanished. "Get out of town or die," a girl's voice begged. "Get out of town or I'm going to kill you, Ms. Capperson. I won't have any other choice."

chapter two

Rhonda handed Rita the note, walked over to the broken window, and peeked out into the snow. The kitchen window looked out into a snow-covered side yard holding a large tree that reminded Rhonda of a tree you would see in some movie. "Any idea who threw that brick?" she asked.

Grabbing a broom from the utility closet, Paula methodically began to sweep up the broken glass with a twisted, angry expression sitting on her face. "No," she answered Rhonda. "But whoever the culprit is will certainly face justice. I assure you of that."

Rita studied the note. It was not handwritten. "It'll be impossible to track this note," she informed Paula. "It was typed up on a computer and sent through a printer."

Paula focused on sweeping up the broken glass. Having an unknown scoundrel destroy the sanctity of her home was very upsetting. Being threatened with death was even more upsetting. Inside the safe harbor of a book, murder was harmless—but in reality, murder was extremely frightening and extremely tangible. "The local police in Mayfield are, to state it plainly: idiots." Paula looked up at Rita. "A few years ago when I visited New York, my purse was stolen. The man who stole it ended up dead. A detective by the name of Conrad Spencer tended to the questions that needed to be asked of me. He was a very nice man. Perhaps I could call—"

"No, bringing in outside people is probably not the best move," Rita told Paula, unaware that this Detective Conrad Spencer was now living in Alaska anyway. "Whoever sent you this note is not a killer—not yet, anyway. We don't need to anger this person and risk escalating the situation." Rita shoved the note into the pocket of her coat. "The person who wrote this note wants you to leave town, Paula."

"Yes, I read the note," Paula reminded Rita in a sharp voice.

Rita looked at Rhonda. "For now, the culprit is remaining nonviolent."

"But for how long?" Rhonda wondered aloud. "If Paula doesn't leave town...who knows? Will they follow through on their threat to kill her?"

Rita studied Paula. "Paula—"

"What choice do I have?" Paula asked as Rita retrieved a white dustpan, swept up the broken glass, and walked over to a silver trash can. "I will leave town and hire an outside detective to track down this...culprit. Once the culprit is apprehended, I will return to Mayfield and continue on with my wedding."

Rhonda shrugged her shoulders at Rita. "If that's the path she wants to take, who are we to argue?"

Rita began to speak but stopped when someone knocked on the back door. She went for her gun but quickly realized she had left it back at the hotel. Bringing a gun into Paula's home seemed inconsiderate and rude. "My gun is back at the hotel," Rita whispered to her sister.

"Not mine," Rhonda whispered back, pulling out a black pistol from her inside coat pocket. "I know what you said," she told Rita in a quick voice, "but I don't feel safe without my gun. Not after falling out of the back of that killer's truck and nearly dying."

Paula, overhearing, made a confused face. "Killer's truck? Nearly dying? What in the world are you talking about, Rhonda?"

"Long story," Rhonda answered as she eased over to the back door and peeked through the dark green curtain covering the oval window attached to the back door. She saw a short, plump man with rosy red cheeks standing in the snow whistling "Winter Wonderland" and looking around as if he didn't have a care in the world. "Uh, I think your fiancé is here, Paula?"

Paula rushed over to the door, peeked out at the man, and nodded. "Yes, that's Oscar," she confirmed and hurried to open the door. "Oscar, what are you doing here?" she asked, confusion on her face.

Oscar Frost—who could have passed for Mickey Rooney's twin—motioned around at the snow and then pointed to the bright red ski jacket and ski cap he was wearing. "I thought we could take a delightful walk in this frozen waterfall, my love. The sweet taste of winter is a delicacy that we must not ignore," he answered Paula in a silly Shakespearean tone.

On any other day, Paula would have accepted Oscar's offer. However, the beautiful snowy day standing before her offered no hint of joy or peace. Her heart was consumed with dread, anger, and fear at the threat to her life. "I informed you that my two friends from Georgia were coming by for afternoon coffee."

"Oh yes, indeed." Oscar beamed. "I wish to invite your friends along as well." Oscar hurried into the kitchen like a child on ice skates and took a quick bow. "Ladies," he said, changing his accent into that of a goofy knight, "my respects."

Rhonda quickly put her gun away and backed up to Rita. "Uh…hello," she said, fighting back laughter. The little squirt standing in Paula's kitchen was certainly eccentric.

"Oh, Oscar, you're dripping snow all over the kitchen floor," Paula complained.

Oscar spotted the broken kitchen window. "Oh dear. I see you have suffered an accident far worse than my snowy boots, my love."

Paula sighed, closed the kitchen door, and put the broom and dustpan away in the utility closet. "Yes, I'm afraid a very hideous fiend sent me a terrible message wrapped around a brick. Very tacky, I must admit."

Rita and Rhonda expected Oscar to stop acting silly and become alarmed at Paula's words. Instead, the little man simply rubbed his frozen chin. "Perhaps a long-lost admirer who does not wish for us to become united in marriage, my love?" he asked.

"I seriously doubt it," Paula replied. "I was warned to leave town or die."

"Oh, such bitter manners," Oscar exclaimed. "Why must the minds of rejected performers send such manners into our beautiful world?"

Rita looked at Rhonda, who shrugged her shoulders. Oscar didn't seem the least bit worried. In fact, the little runt seemed to be off in a world that only his lost mind could understand. "A threat like that is to be taken very seriously, Mr. Frost," she said.

"Oh, indeed," Oscar agreed. He yanked off the red ski cap and presented a head of thinning red hair. "My apologies for allowing sheer ignorance to speak for me."

"Uh...no problem," Rhonda said and looked at Paula. Paula was studying the kitchen floor, obviously ashamed that the man she was going to marry was making a fool of himself. "I...uh, Paula, maybe you should call someone to repair the kitchen window? All that cold air is coming inside."

"Of course," Paula said. "I will use the telephone in the living room. Please excuse me." Paula exited the kitchen on lonely legs, leaving Oscar Frost to entertain the two beautiful sisters.

Oscar watched Paula leave the kitchen and then looked at Rhonda and Rita. His eyes glowed, and in a flash his face changed. "Hey, you two are sure cute," he said and tossed a flirty wink into the air. "Paula didn't tell me that she was inviting two babes over for coffee."

"Babes?" Rhonda repeated.

"Hey, hey," Rita snapped, "you're engaged to Paula, you jerk."

Oscar threw a dismissive hand into the air. "I'd ditch that old rug for you girls in a second." He winked at Rita. "What are you doing tonight, hot stuff? I know a good restaurant."

"Knock it off." Rita slapped Oscar on the arm.

"We have a Casanova on our hands." Rhonda rolled her eyes.

"I'm forty-four, girls. I don't have time to hand out roses," Oscar explained and winked at Rhonda. "How about a little kiss?"

"Hey," Rita snapped again and slapped Oscar across his face. "Knock it off before I stick your face in the snow."

Oscar felt his face with a gloved hand. "I'll never wash this face again," he sighed.

"Good grief," Rita exclaimed. "Rhonda...kick him out. I'm going to check on Paula. Holy moly, I can't believe she's marrying this guy."

Rhonda watched Rita storm out of the kitchen. Oscar grinned. "Now that we're alone, hot stuff, maybe we can share a little kiss?"

Rhonda yanked out her gun. "Out," she told Oscar.

Oscar grinned, probably not believing the gun was real. "Playing hard to get will only make the heart more determined, my love," he said.

"Out," Rhonda warned again and pushed Oscar toward the back door. "Go soak your head in the snow for a while."

"My love for you will melt the snow and turn it into a river of romance," Oscar promised.

Rhonda rolled her eyes. "You're supposed to be marrying Paula, you jerk."

Oscar slowly opened the back door. "Marriage can be for love or for convenience," he told Rhonda in a goofy voice. "I will return, my love, tonight, for pizza and root beer, at the stroke of seven."

"I can hardly wait," Rhonda muttered as she slammed the kitchen door shut. She heard Oscar kick his heels together and exclaim that he was in love. "Paula wasn't kidding when she said that little fart was eccentric," she said. She slowly put her gun away and went to find Rita and Paula.

Paula was sitting on a fancy white and pink couch resting in a living room that was far too fancy to even step in let alone rest in. "Yes, yes, my kitchen window," she said, speaking into an antique phone. "Two hours? Yes, I suppose that will have to do. I'll be waiting." Paula set the phone down. "The window repair man will be arriving in two hours," she said and looked up at Rhonda. "Where is Oscar?"

"Uh...he went to play in the snow," Rhonda told Paula, giving Rita an "oh boy" look.

Paula sighed. "Oscar flirted with you, didn't he?" she asked. "He flirts with every pretty face he sees."

"Then why marry him?" Rita asked, confused.

"Rita," Paula explained, looking around the fancy living room, "I am forty-four years old. I am lonely. I admit that Oscar isn't...ideal, but he is willing to call me his wife." Paula motioned at the living room. "When I sit in this room late in the evening alone, listening to my classical music or simply reading, I can feel a thick loneliness in the air. The loneliness grabs at my tortured heart and begs for companionship. I'm sure you two do not understand what I mean?"

"Sure we do," Rhonda spoke up. "Paula, Rita and I aren't married, you know. We spend some lonely nights in our kitchen back home playing board games...wondering when Mr. Right might come along."

Rita looked deep into Paula's eyes. "Paula, marriage is a very serious commitment. As lonely as life can become at times, a person shouldn't settle for someone who isn't right for them simply because they are lonely."

"Rita," Paula said and gently patted Rita's hand, "a mirror smiles when you gaze into it. A mirror cries when I scare its face. You have the luxury of choosing because you are beautiful. I, on the other hand, do not. Oscar Frost may be the only man who will ever desire to marry me." Paula looked down at her hands. "Now, enough with that. We need to focus on the threat at hand."

"Well, leaving town and hiring an outside detective to find the person who threw that brick through your window isn't going to help," Rhonda pointed out. She walked over to the glossy brown piano sitting in the far corner and studied it. "You could have a slew of detectives, Paula, but they're not going to locate the person who smashed your kitchen window."

"Rhonda is right," Rita pointed out and locked eyes with her sister. Rhonda winced but then slowly and painfully nodded. "Paula, with your permission, Rhonda and I would like to accept your case and see what we can find."

"Uh...yeah, sure," Rhonda told Paula. "I mean...what are friends for, right?" she asked as her mind began calculating how many more minutes she had to spend in Vermont before she could return home to Clovedale Falls.

Paula hesitated. "I wouldn't want you two to face any danger," she said. "From my understanding, you are both retired."

"Retirement doesn't seem to be agreeing with us," Rhonda told Paula. She walked over to a wooden bookshelf and studied a row of classic novels. "Rita and I have been dealing with some rough characters lately. I'm sure we can handle your case," she explained. She tossed a quick eye at Rita. "I mean, we're probably dealing with...I don't know...maybe some kid you flunked in math?"

"One of my students?" Paula's eyes widened in shock. "Why, my students respect me," she insisted. "Yes, I am firm and very hard, but my students respect that. Why, the mere thought of one of my students performing such a hideous act is ludicrous."

"Paula," Rita cut in, "a professional killer wouldn't throw a brick through a window," she pointed out. "I have to agree with my sister. The first place I would look would be toward the classroom you teach in."

"Why...impossible," Paula exclaimed. She stood up and began pacing around the living room. "In all the years I have been teaching at the private academy, not one single student has ever stepped out of line. The students there are raised prim and proper. They are the future leaders of tomorrow and are trained from a young age not to resort to such childish acts of hatred."

Rita slowly stood up. "Regardless," she said, forcing her voice to become tough, "it wouldn't hurt for you to give us the names of all of your students."

"Absolutely not," Paula refused. "Rita, I expected better from you."

"Are you kidding us?" Rhonda asked. "You're the one marrying a Casanova clown, you bitter old prune."

"Well, I..." Paula turned red. "So much for friendship. You both may leave my home now."

Rita looked at Rhonda. Rhonda winced and shrugged her shoulders. "Come on," Rita said and walked out of the living room. Rhonda followed. Paula remained in the living room. "Nice going."

"That old prune insulted you," Rhonda said as she snatched open the front door and stepped out into the snow.

"I'm sorry, Rita, but you're my sister. Nobody talks to you that way."

Rita stepped out into the snow with her sister and closed the front door. "I know...and thank you," she said in a loving voice. "I suppose Paula is a very difficult person to understand and accept."

Rhonda looked around at the snow-covered neighborhood lined with fancy two-story homes sitting on snow-covered lawns. "She probably made one of her students mad, Sis."

"That's the area I'm leaning toward, too." Rita nodded. "Well...since we have been kicked out and have time on our hands...lunch?"

"You bet." Rhonda beamed. "Let that old prune deal with her own problems. Come on." Rhonda took Rita's hand and walked her down the snow-soaked walkway. Seconds later, Oscar appeared behind them.

"Ladies...lunch?" Oscar asked and grinned from ear to ear.

Rita and Rhonda looked at each other and rolled their eyes. They doused Oscar with snow, ran to the parked gray rental SUV, and dived inside.

Rita called Billy from inside a warm café that smelled of fresh coffee, hot flapjacks, and delicious muffins. "Hey, Billy," she said, sitting with her sister at a round table covered with a white and red checkered tablecloth, "it's Rita. How are you?"

Billy was standing inside the barn fussing up a storm. "I'd be doing a lot better if my blasted milk cow wouldn't have gotten loose somehow and wandered off. How in the world that cow escaped is beyond me." Billy shook his head. "This is the fourth time she's wandered off this year. Makes me wonder why I even keep her around."

Rita smiled and quickly glanced out the oval window next

to the table and watched a heavy snow fall. "Have you gotten any snow yet?"

"It spit a little snow a little while ago but not enough to cover the ground," Billy explained and shrugged his shoulders at Zach. "Best go check the orchards again," he said. "I'll be joining you shortly." Zach nodded and walked out into a freezing rain. "How is your trip going?"

"Uh...eventful," Rita told Billy, still watching the snow fall.

Rhonda rolled her eyes and pointed to another table. Oscar was sitting there. He waved a happy hand in the air. "Eventful isn't the word," she sighed. Oscar stopped waving and winked. "Oh brother."

Rita ignored Oscar. The little squirt was harmless. "To be honest, Billy...the trip hasn't exactly turned out the way we planned."

Billy checked the empty milk stall and shook his head. "Dumb cow," he mumbled and then focused back on Rita. "Why ain't your trip going good?"

Rita patiently explained about Paula and then told him about the brick being thrown through the kitchen window. "Paula kicked us out of her home when we suggested one of her students might be responsible."

A few patrons, mostly old men sitting around drinking coffee and reading newspapers, seemed oblivious to Rita and Rhonda. However, it was clear that the patrons were not pleased to see Oscar Frost. The one person who seemed happy to see him was a waitress in her mid-forties who seemed to have a good sense of humor. The waitress was new to town and was just happy to have a job. The waitress was very pretty, but, sadly, she didn't speak in a way that showed grand intelligence. "More coffee?" she asked, approaching Rita's and Rhonda's table.

"Sure." Rhonda raised her brown coffee cup up into the air. "Rita?" Rita shook her head no.

"I just love the snow," the waitress said in a cheerful voice. "I grew up in Southern California. I never saw snow."

Rhonda spotted a name tag sitting on the waitress's uniform shirt. "Uh...I guess it doesn't snow much in that area of the country, huh, Maple?"

Maple Potter shook her head no. "Not much," she said, showing her ditzy side. She finished filling Rhonda's coffee cup and glanced down at the brown work uniform she was wearing. "I look so silly in this thing. And my hair," Maple motioned up to her lovely blonde hair, "looks awful today."

"You look fine." Rhonda smiled.

"More coffee, my love," Oscar called out.

Maple smiled. "He's so silly," she giggled and hurried away.

"Oh brother." Rhonda almost vomited.

Rita shook her head. "Anyway," she said into the phone, "looks like Rhonda and I will be cutting our trip short, Billy."

Billy walked out of his barn, ignored the freezing rain, and looked around. "Stupid cow," he fussed under his breath and then told Rita: "There ain't really no need to rush back. It's cold and rainy and—" Before Billy could finish his sentence, he spotted Jose and Zach appearing over a small hill. Jose was pulling his milk cow with a rope. "Well now. Jose done went and found that silly cow for me," Billy exclaimed in a happy voice.

"That's good to hear, Billy." Rita smiled at Rhonda. "Jose found the missing milk cow," she whispered. "Such adventures are taking place back home."

Rhonda grinned. She could imagine Billy getting excited over finding a missing milk cow. "And just think, we're sitting in a warm café waiting to eat a delicious lunch. We miss out on all the fun."

Rita laughed. "I guess we do," she said and turned her attention back to Billy. "Well, Billy, I guess I'll say goodbye and let you put your cow away."

"I'm going to lock that cow in a cage this time," Billy promised Rita and began to say goodbye. Then, for no reason he could really understand, Billy looked around his rainy farm and sighed. "I reckon I wouldn't mind taking a trip," he confessed. "Billy Northfield loves his farm, but on days like today, he sure could use a break."

Rita felt a surge of happiness enter her heart. "Billy, why don't you fly up to Vermont?" she asked. "We can rent a cabin —one of those large ones with three or four bedrooms—and spend a week in the snow?"

Rhonda looked at Rita with curious eyes. Rita blushed. She wasn't acting very practical and was actually feeling like a silly schoolgirl. But so what?

Billy walked back into his barn and rubbed the back of his neck. "You mean go up there into Yankee territory?" he asked in an uncertain voice. "Why, I heard they don't serve sweet tea and don't even know what a grit is. And I sure ain't starting my morning without a bowl of buttered cheese grits, no sir."

Rita giggled. "I'm sure we can locate some grits," she promised. "And I assure you, Billy, the people in Vermont are very friendly." Rita spotted Oscar flirting with poor Maple. Maple didn't seem to mind. The woman had no clue that Oscar was trying to romance her. In Maple's mind, she simply saw a friendly customer who might leave a decent tip. "Well…most people."

Rhonda glanced toward Oscar and rolled her eyes. "Can you imagine Billy meeting that little runt?" she whispered. "Why, Billy would hogtie him."

Rita giggled again. "Probably," she said.

Billy heard the sound of Rita's sweet giggle and nearly melted. Why in the world a beautiful woman like Rita Knight was showing him attention he just didn't know. "Well, I reckon I can let Zach be in charge for a bit," he said, spotting

Jose and Zach walking into the barn. "I'll leave Jose at his side to watch him."

"Does that mean you'll fly up?" Rita asked in a hopeful voice.

Billy rubbed the back of his neck again. "Naw, be best if I drove up. Chester will want to come," he said. "He's already putting up a fuss because it's cold and rainy. That dog can never be happy with the weather. It's a wonder I even keep him around."

Rita pictured Billy pulling into the small town of Mayfield, Vermont—a fancy little town full of fancy vehicles and fancy homes. She saw Billy walking around in his overalls with Chester at his side. "Well...if you think that's best."

Billy debated. "I reckon I can leave Chester with Zach. Those two seem to get along well enough," he said. "And I reckon it wouldn't kill me to get on one of them airplanes... but my daddy said man ain't meant to fly, no sir." Billy shook his head. "I reckon I'll just stay to my original thought and drive up to Yankee territory in my truck with Chester at my side."

Rita smiled. "Okay, Billy."

"Reckon if I leave in the next couple of hours I should be getting to your location in a couple of days."

"Mayfield is very close to the Canadian border, Billy," Rita explained. "Give yourself at least three days to get here."

Jose and Zach looked at Billy. The large, lazy milk cow standing next to them let out an angry moo. Billy told the cow to shut it and threatened to cook it for supper. Of course, deep down, Billy loved his old milk cow and wouldn't never harm it. He just liked to fuss. "Okay, three days," Billy agreed. "Chester and me will leave shortly."

"When you arrive in Mayfield, drive to the Snowdrift Inn," Rita said, beaming. "Rhonda and I are staying in room 111."

"Room 111...Snowdrift Inn...got it," Billy told Rita. "I best put this old cow up and get to packing."

"Okay, call me tonight." Rita smiled and ended the call. "Billy is going to drive up."

"I see." Rhonda grinned at Rita.

Rita blushed. "Is it that obvious?" Rhonda nodded. "I'm making a dummy of myself, aren't I?"

"Of course not," Rhonda said. "Billy is a nice guy. You could do a lot worse, Sis. And to be honest, I don't think you could do much better."

"Billy isn't a suit-and-tie man," Rita replied. She picked up her coffee and took a sip. "We aren't exactly ideal mates. He's a...well, he's a..."

"Hillbilly farmer and you're a practical woman from Atlanta," Rhonda finished for Rita.

"Well...yes," Rita confessed.

"Sis, Billy may be a hillbilly farmer, but the guy isn't stupid," Rhonda pointed out in a loving voice. "Billy handled himself really well in Nevada."

"He saved my life."

Rhonda nodded. "If you're searching for a snotty stockbroker to marry, Sis, then you're going to miss out on a whole lot of happiness...happiness Billy has to offer."

Rita pictured Billy walking into a sleepy kitchen and fixing himself a bowl of cheese grits. Next, she saw the kitchen turn into a fancy restaurant filled with men wearing suits. "I'd rather be in Billy's kitchen," she admitted to Rhonda.

Rhonda began to reply but stopped when the front door to the café opened. A thin man in his early fifties walked in wearing a brown sheriff's coat and hat. "Hey, it's Barney Fife," Rhonda joked.

Rita looked over and spotted the sheriff. He looked straight at Rita and walked over to her table. "Ms. Knight?" he asked and then looked at Rhonda. "Ms. Knight?"

Rita and Rhonda nodded their heads. "Yes."

"My name is Sheriff Ralph O'Neil," he said in a squeaky voice. "Uh..." Sheriff O'Neil studied the warm café with nervous eyes. "I'm afraid...your friend Paula Capperson is dead. Uh...Mrs. Mayberry at the Snowdrift Inn told me you were having lunch here."

Rita looked at Rhonda. Rhonda put down her coffee. The situation had just turned very serious—and tragic. "We just left Paula's home about an hour ago," Rita told Sheriff O'Neil.

"I know," Sheriff O'Neil replied. "Paula Capperson called my office and put in a complaint. She said someone threw a brick through her window and left a threatening message. She explained that you two were present at the time."

Rita could clearly see that Sheriff O'Neil was a nervous man. "We were there." She nodded and then remembered she had the threatening note in her coat pocket. "Oh, I forgot to give the note back to Paula," she said. She quickly retrieved the note and handed it to Sheriff O'Neil. "This is the note that was attached to the brick."

Rhonda looked at Oscar. He was feeding a fat cheeseburger into his mouth without a care in the world. "Well, one thing is for certain, that little runt isn't the killer," she pointed out. "He followed us from Paula's house to our hotel and then followed us here."

Sheriff O'Neil looked at Oscar with disgusted eyes. Oscar waved at him. "Get over here," the sheriff said. Oscar shrugged his shoulders, wiped his mouth with a napkin, and made his way over to Sheriff O'Neil. "Oscar, Paula Capperson is dead. Stan Hillside found her body."

Oscar slowly folded his arms. "Ah, such a loss we have encountered," he said in his goofy Shakespearean tone.

"Will you knock it off," Rhonda snapped. "A woman is dead...a woman you were supposed to be marrying, you little squirt. Show some respect."

Oscar shrugged. "I did not love the recently departed," he

stated. "Our marriage was one of convenience rather than love. My heart cannot grieve for nothing more. Now, if you will excuse me, my cheeseburger is waiting."

"Wait a minute," Sheriff O'Neil insisted in his squeaky voice. "Oscar Frost, you were the closest person to Paula Capperson. You have to know something."

Rita studied Oscar's eyes. The man, sadly, didn't have a clue to offer. "He doesn't know anything, Sheriff," she pointed out. "Take a hike, mister."

"Oh, my sweet love, don't let the death of another woman cause bitterness between us," Oscar pleaded. "Our love must carry on." Oscar tossed a wink at Rita and went back to his table without a care in the world.

"No wonder he's so disliked," Rhonda said in a disgusted voice.

"Well, I guess from his viewpoint, you can't really blame him," Rita pointed out. "Paula did confess that she was marrying Oscar out of convenience, too. You can't blame the guy for not breaking into tears."

"I guess not," Rhonda agreed. She looked up at Sheriff O'Neil. "What can we do to help, Sheriff?"

Sheriff O'Neil nervously placed his hands into the pockets of his coat. "Paula told me you two are retired homicide detectives from Atlanta. Is that right?"

"Yes," Rita confirmed. "My sister and I are retired."

Sheriff O'Neil glanced around the café again. "Ladies, Mayfield is a very small town and I'm a simple sheriff. I only became sheriff because the last sheriff, who was my brother, broke his leg and I was asked to take his place. I sold insurance before that. I don't know the first thing about...murder."

"We do," Rhonda assured him. "Sheriff, where is Paula Capperson's body at this very second?"

"Where else?" Sheriff O'Neil said. "I left the body at the

murder scene with Stan Hillside. Stan didn't want to stay with the body, but I insisted."

"Who is Stan Hillside?" Rita asked.

"Window repair man," Sheriff O'Neil explained. "Stan told me he showed up sooner than expected to fix the window."

Rita looked at Rhonda and stood up. "Okay, Sis, looks like our vacation just turned sour. We have work to do."

Rhonda grabbed her coat and looked over at Oscar, who was back flirting with poor Maple as if nothing at all had happened. "We're not through with him," she told Rita. "Maybe Oscar doesn't know something…consciously. But maybe Paula said something to him that might be of importance to us?"

Rita agreed. "Okay, Sheriff, we're ready."

Sheriff O'Neil nodded and left the café with Rita and Rhonda following close behind. Oscar remained in his seat and continued to flirt with Maple. Far away, a very scared seventeen-year-old girl ran into her bedroom, slammed the door, and covered her eyes with shaky hands.

"I didn't mean to kill her…oh, I wanted to…but I didn't mean to…" the girl cried. "Oh, Daddy is going to murder me." The poor, distraught girl had no idea that the real killer was loose.

chapter three

The sheriff, followed by Rhonda and Rita, walked into Paula's kitchen where an old man with thick gray hair stood next to a body covered with a green blanket. "I put this blanket over her," Stan Hillside spoke up in an uneasy voice. He shoved his hands into the pockets of his gray work coat and eased over to the back door. "These two women must be the cops you told me about."

"I'm Rita Knight, and this is Rhonda Knight," Rita told Stan.

Rhonda pulled off her gloves and placed them into the right pocket of her coat. "The sheriff told us you were the one who found Paula Capperson's body." Stan nodded. "Okay, Mr. Hillside, please tell us the events that took place from the moment you arrived up until the moment you discovered the body."

Stan leaned back against the kitchen door. "I figured it was going to take me at least two hours to arrive here," he explained. "I was scheduled to go to another residence and replace a storm window. I'm a bachelor, and the residence I was scheduled to go to…well, it's no secret Ms. Owens and I have coffee together." Stan kept his eyes on the blanket. "As it turned out, the storm window didn't need replacing. Ms. Owens just wanted to have coffee with me."

"You two should get married," Sheriff O'Neil told Stan as he eased around Rita and Rhonda and looked down at the blanket-covered body.

Stan shrugged. "I'm not ready yet," he explained and nodded at the body. "While I was talking with Ms. Owens," he continued, "Ms. Capperson called me again and insisted that I arrive earlier than scheduled because her house was freezing. She sounded very angry, and I knew she wasn't going to stop calling me until I caved. Ms. Owens urged me to come and fix the broken window so she could go back to her home and we could drink our coffee in peace."

"What time did you leave Ms. Owens?" Rita asked. She looked at the kitchen window and saw snow whispering through the broken glass.

Stan checked his watch and gave a time. "Ms. Owens lives about five minutes from here," he pointed out. "Even with the snow, I got here in good time. When I arrived, I decided to walk around to the kitchen and examine the broken window. There's really no sense in having a homeowner go through an entire story about how the window was broken. A broken window is a broken window." Stan raised his eyes. "Ms. Owens was expecting me and all I wanted to do was get a fix on the window, replace it, hand a bill to Ms. Capperson, and be on my way."

"How did you locate the body?" Rita asked.

"By looking through the broken window," Stan told Rita in an obvious voice. "I peered through the window and saw Ms. Capperson lying face down on the kitchen floor. I thought she'd had a heart attack."

"What did you do?" Rhonda asked.

"I ran around to the back door," Stan explained. "I was prepared to kick the back door open, but the door was unlocked. I ran to Ms. Capperson and..." Stan shook his head. "When I rolled her body over to check to see if she was breathing or had a pulse, I saw her neck...and I realized that she had been...strangled."

Rita bent down, pulled back the cover hiding Paula's body, and studied her neck. Rhonda joined her. "She's been strangled," Rita confirmed.

Rhonda nodded. "The killer used a rope instead of his hands," she noted.

Sheriff O'Neil dared to venture over and peek down. He saw an ugly red scar racing around Paula's neck. "How do you know a rope was used?"

"See how wide the strangle line is?" Rita asked. "It's too wide to be, oh, fish string for example." Rita sighed. "Let's check under her fingernails. Maybe she managed to scratch the killer and got some of his DNA under her nails."

Rhonda nodded and checked Paula's right hand while Rita checked her left. "I have what appear to be rope fibers."

"Same here," Rita said. "Paula was grabbing at the rope instead of the killer." Rita bent down and sniffed Paula's dress. "No scent other than her perfume."

Rhonda examined Paula's shoes. "Left shoe is nearly off her foot. Right shoe is halfway off. Looks like she was attacked from behind and yanked backward."

Sheriff O'Neil watched Rita and Rhonda investigate the body with amazed eyes. "What does this mean?" he asked.

Rita checked Paula's dress. "No tears in the dress," she pointed out. "Pockets are clean."

Rhonda felt Paula's hair. "Hair is a bit damp," she said and then felt Paula's shoes. "Shoes are still a bit damp, too," she noted.

Rita looked at the back door and saw Paula's coat hanging on a wooden coat rack. She stood up and checked the coat. "Coat is dry," she said and then focused back on Paula's body. "From the position of the body, it looks like she was trying to exit the kitchen when she died."

Rhonda agreed. "The killer came through the back door," she said. "Could be Paula tried to run?"

"Could be, but then why..." Rita bit down on her lower lip and studied the kitchen. "Could be the killer yanked Paula outside into the snow but Paula somehow managed to get back inside?"

"That would explain the damp hair and shoes along with the dry coat." Rhonda covered Paula's body with the green blanket. "Could be the killer was intending to kidnap her, Sis, but when Paula put up a fight, she was strangled with a rope that might have been intended to tie her hands together?"

Rita agreed. "Whoever killed Paula was obviously much stronger than she was," she continued. "And Paula wouldn't have opened the back door to just anyone—"

"Unless she thought it was him," Rhonda said and pointed at Stan.

"Hey, wait a minute," Stan exclaimed in a panicked voice, "I didn't kill Ms. Capperson."

"Of course not," Sheriff O'Neil told Stan. He looked at Rita and Rhonda with worried eyes. "Right?" he asked.

Rita nodded. "We're not accusing you, Mr. Hillside," she promised. "We're just pointing out that Paula wouldn't have opened the back door to just anyone, not after receiving a threatening letter."

"The only problem is," Rhonda pointed out, "Paula claimed she was a loner, which narrows down the list of suspects to...zero."

"Well, except for her students," Rita reminded Rhonda. "As well as her co-workers."

Sheriff O'Neil eased over to Stan. "The residents of Mayfield are certainly going to be very upset."

"Don't I know it," Stan agreed. "But Ralph, someone killed Ms. Capperson," he added in an uneasy voice. "And whoever killed this woman is out in the snow, free as a bird.

Might be good to have people in our sleepy town get upset. It'll make them cautious."

"I know, I know," Sheriff O'Neil said and rubbed his tired nose. "Weather report said the snow is going to get heavier and stay with us a few more days."

"An early winter is setting in all over the country," Stan said. "I've seen it happen before and so have you."

"The last thing we need while looking for a killer is all this snow," Sheriff O'Neil complained.

"Sheriff, you better have the body taken to the local morgue," Rita ordered. "In the meantime, if you would like, my sister and I can start conducting an...unofficial investigation."

"Starting at the private school Paula was teaching at," Rhonda added.

"Schools are out today," Sheriff O'Neil told Rhonda. "It's Sunday."

"Yeah, that's right," Rhonda said. "I guess we'll have to wait until tomorrow."

"In the meantime," Rita said, nodding at Paula's body, "an official autopsy is going to have to be conducted by the state criminal lab. Sheriff, you better get on the phone and contact the state."

Sheriff O'Neil moaned. "I have a very bad dislike for suits," he mumbled. "What choice do I have? I have rules to follow."

Stan nodded toward the back door. "Can I leave now?"

"You better go down to the sheriff's station and write out an official statement," Rhonda told Stan. "It's standard procedure, nothing major."

"I understand," Stan told Rhonda in a grateful voice.

"Go on down to the station, Stan. Someone there will help you," Sheriff O'Neil said. Stan nodded and left the kitchen through the back door. "Okay," he told Rita and Rhonda, "what else do I need to do?"

"Follow your SOP," Rita told Sheriff O'Neil in a professional voice. "My sister and I will stand back in the shadows and look around. Tomorrow we'll go up to the school Paula taught at and see what we can discover."

Sheriff O'Neil looked worried. "Do you ladies honestly believe one of Ms. Capperson's students killed her?"

"It's possible," Rhonda said. "It's also possible that whoever killed Paula Capperson panicked." She looked down at the body. "The killer may or may not have intentionally left the body behind."

"Teenagers panic very easily," Rita pointed out. "A trained killer wouldn't leave a body behind unless the intention was to leave a message. I can't seem to locate a message in this kitchen, Sheriff."

Sheriff O'Neil shook his head with worry. "I hope you two ladies are wrong," he said, "because if you aren't, the town of Mayfield is going to erupt." Sheriff O'Neil walked to the back door and looked out into the snowy backyard. "Ladies," he said, "Mayfield is a sleepy town full of young families. We have a Dairy Queen and drive-in...not much different from the South." Sheriff O'Neil kept his eyes on the snow. "The private school up on Snowpine Hill is the only fancy piece of candy Mayfield has. People from all over the world send their children to that school. Why? I honestly don't know. The school is cold, and the staff is very hard and unfriendly. If one of Paula Capperson's students did murder her, we're talking about dealing with parents who have more money than sense...powerful people."

Rhonda glanced at Rita. Rita was staring at Sheriff O'Neil. "I think we're starting to understand your concern," she said.

Sheriff O'Neil turned away from the snow, looking at Rita and Rhonda with worried eyes. "Mayfield actually depends on certain income benefits the private school provides," he explained. "Since it's a private school, it pays property taxes, which, along with other benefits, helps Mayfield."

"Such as?" Rhonda asked.

"For starters, my company provides the fire insurance," Sheriff O'Neil explained. "Stan installed all the windows. Steve takes care of the landscaping and snow."

"Steve?" Rhonda asked.

"The man who owns the local landscaping business," Sheriff O'Neil explained. "Andrew and his sons take care of the building maintenance—cleaning and what have you," he continued, speaking as if Rita and Rhonda knew the names he was speaking, as if they knew the people the names belonged to on a personal basis. "Nate installed the central air and heating, Brad and his sons put on the roof, Phil's construction company built the school." Sheriff O'Neil rubbed his neck. "That school created and still creates a lot of employment for this town. And, as I said, the property taxes the school pays help keep local property taxes down and allow people to pour more money into the local economy. Mayfield has a decent mayor who fights to keep the community traditional and, as much as possible, low cost."

"We can appreciate that, Sheriff," Rita promised, "however, a murder has taken place and justice must be dispensed."

Sheriff O'Neil nodded. "I understand that, ladies," he promised, "and I'm going to do everything I can within my power, and the power of my office—even though I'm not really a qualified sheriff—to make sure Ms. Capperson receives justice. I only wish you two weren't so confident that the murderer is residing up at the private school."

"We could be wrong," Rhonda said.

Sheriff O'Neil shook his head. "You don't believe that. I may not be a qualified sheriff, but I know when a person is going to buy an insurance policy and when they're not just by looking into their eyes. Your eyes are telling me that I have a lot of dreading to do."

Rita bit down on her lower lip. "Sheriff," she began to

speak but stopped when Oscar Frost stuck his head through the back door.

"I came to pay my respects to the recently departed," Oscar announced. He looked down at the kitchen floor, spotted Paula, and let out a cheesy sigh. "Oh, sweet woman, our love was only that of a single drop of rain. Oh, how the years could have turned into a river of—"

"Oh, zip it," Rhonda snapped. "You're going to make me vomit."

Oscar shrugged. "Okay," he said, speaking in his simple voice, "the real reason I came over is because I don't want to be accused of killing the old broad. Sure, she has a nice home and a nice retirement package, but that's not worth going to prison over. And besides, that's all moot since the lady and I had yet to tie the knot."

"Can you believe this runt?" Rhonda asked Rita in a disgusted voice.

Sheriff O'Neil looked at Oscar with cold eyes. "People in Mayfield avoid this guy like he is a disease."

"Your insult will not get you reelected," Oscar retorted in a sour voice. "I shall vote for your opponent."

"I have no opponent, you dimwit," Sheriff O'Neil snapped. "No one ever runs against my brother and as soon as his leg heals, I'm going back to selling insurance."

"Speaking of your brother," Rita said in a quick voice, "you should contact him."

"My brother is currently out of town," Sheriff O'Neil told Rita. "And, well, I would contact him, but after he broke his leg he had a nervous breakdown. His wife took him to Florida."

"Why did your brother have a nervous breakdown?" Rhonda asked. "Breaking your leg is nothing to freak out over."

"You don't know the sheriff's...shall we say...nervous brother." Oscar grinned. He slapped his arms together and leaned back against the kitchen door. "The man jumps at his own shadow."

"Shut up," Sheriff O'Neil warned.

Oscar ignored Sheriff O'Neil. "The poor man slipped on an icy sidewalk and broke his leg. His gun went off and shot out a car window and nearly killed poor Mrs. Branton. Mrs. Branton's husband threatened to kill the good sheriff, who, in return, crumbled under all the drama and ran away to the warm shores of sunny Florida."

Rita looked at Rhonda. All Rhonda could do was shrug her shoulders. Mayfield sure seemed like it was a town full of...crooks. And to make matters worse, Billy Northfield was on his way up from Georgia. How in the world was Billy going to deal with the town of Mayfield, Vermont?

Rita and Rhonda walked into the small but cozy mayor's office. "Please sit," a short, chubby man wearing a simple gray suit said. The man suspiciously resembled Oscar Frost.

"Thank you," Rita said and politely sat down in a gray cushioned chair resting in front of a modest brown desk. Rhonda sat down next to her and glanced around the office. She spotted a brown carpet that appeared old enough to be called vintage, a wooden filing cabinet, a bookshelf, two fake plants, and an oval window covered over with dark blue drapes. The interior design of the office was about what she had expected to find.

Mayor Barney White sat down in an uncomfortable-looking wooden chair and quickly folded his hands together. "I'm very pleased that you ladies agreed to see me on such short notice. When I heard that Paula Capperson had been killed, I became very distraught."

Rhonda focused her eyes back on Mayor White. "Uh... forgive me for asking, but are you related to..."

"Oscar Frost?" Mayor White asked, his face falling.

"Well, yes. You two do favor," Rhonda said.

"Oscar Frost is my first cousin," Mayor White confessed. "But make no mistake, ladies, that swamp turtle and I are far from being...friendly toward one another. I couldn't stand Oscar when we were children, and I dislike him even more as an adult."

Rita looked at Rhonda. Rhonda nodded. Oscar Frost surely didn't have any friends. "Mayor," Rita said, "my sister and I are officially retired and have no authority to—"

"I understand," Mayor White said, quickly interrupting Rita. "That's why I wanted to speak to you as soon as possible."

"I'm afraid we don't understand," Rita said, glancing over at her sister.

Mayor White leaned forward, snatched a piece of peppermint candy out of a crystal dish, and threw it into his mouth. "You have both met Sheriff O'Neil."

"Yes," Rita and Rhonda confirmed.

Mayor White nodded. "Ralph is a good man—one of the best," he said in a kind voice. "However, Ralph is no crime fighter. And right now, that's the way I would prefer it."

"Why?" Rita asked, studying Mayor White's worried face. She had a bad feeling what direction Mayor White was attempting to ease into.

"Ladies," Mayor White said, "Ralph told me you two suspect that a student at Green Valley Private Academy could be the responsible culprit?"

Rita and Rhonda glanced at each other and then simply shrugged their shoulders. "We suspect that may be the case," Rita spoke.

Mayor White chewed on his peppermint. "Ladies," he said, trying to speak in a careful and intelligent voice, "Green Valley Private Academy is home to some of the world's richest people. Tuition alone is seventy-five thousand dollars a year."

Rhonda whistled. "That's a lot of dough."

"Yes, it is," Mayor White agreed. "The academy sits on five hundred and twenty acres of lush land. The building, even though modern, is large enough to house an army." Mayor White reached for another piece of candy. "The original building caught fire and burned down three years ago. Phil Canton was hired to build the new school," he said. "Many local businesses were also hired on."

"Yes, Sheriff O'Neil told us that," Rita told Mayor White.

"Then he must have told you that the academy still isn't complete yet," Mayor White explained. "Phil is constantly working on some portion of the school. There's always a plumbing or electrical issue that has to be worked on. Besides that, the headmaster is constantly demanding changes be made to the original design—which is actually beneficial because as long as there is work at the academy, the locals can earn an income." Mayor White popped another piece of peppermint into his mouth. "Winters are very rough in this part of the country, and work becomes extremely scarce. Do you ladies understand what I'm hinting at?"

"Yeah," Rhonda said, "you don't want us upsetting the piggy bank."

Mayor White coughed, shifted uncomfortably in his seat, and slowly nodded. "The academy is a...very important item to Mayfield," he confessed. "Phil hired every free hand in town and then was forced to hire outside contractors. People in Mayfield have had three very comfortable winters which, in return, has kept small businesses afloat and unemployment rates down, as well as the welfare lines. The local churches haven't had to help people with oil, rent, or groceries these past three winters. And while it may be true that the academy isn't employing as many locals as before, many local residents are still receiving income."

"But if we aim Paula Capperson's murder at the academy, we could ruffle some very important feathers, right?" Rhonda asked. "Certain rich parents could pull their precious marshmallows out of Mayfield. And if that happens, Mayfield will take a financial hit to the nose, right?"

"I'm afraid you're absolutely correct," Mayor White confessed, "which is why I must ask you ladies to have no further involvement in this matter. I must insist, as a matter of fact. I know this might make you think very badly of me, but I must do what is good for the town."

Rita understood Mayor White's position. However, Paula Capperson had been, if not a close friend, then someone she had known. The woman may have been a cold fish, but she certainly deserved to have her death properly investigated. Rita knew if she left Mayfield without carrying out a promised duty, she would never be able to forgive herself. "Mayor, officially, you can prevent us from further involvement. But unofficially, my sister and I have as much right to remain in Mayfield as you do."

"And unofficially," Rhonda added, "my sister and I might visit Green Valley Academy because…who knows, if we ever have children, we might want to send them there someday."

Mayor White stared at Rita and Rhonda. He saw determination rise up in the faces of two beautiful women. "I wish I had a mean bone in my body," he said, "but I don't. If I did, I would kick the both of you out into the snow."

"Mayor," Rita said, remaining calm, "Paula Capperson deserves to have justice carried out in her name. She was murdered. Justice outweighs personal obligations."

"Trying to keep the food stamp lines down during the winter months is not a personal obligation…it's a public duty."

"And so is obtaining justice," Rita said in a stern voice. "I can understand your concerns, Mayor White, and I can even appreciate them. But when a person substitutes justice for dollar signs, he or she perverts their very soul."

"Attempting to make sure my town survives isn't—"

Rita stood up. "I realize what you're trying to relay to me, Mayor White, but a woman has been murdered and justice must be carried out."

Mayor White knew Rita was right, of course, but he had the good of the town to consider. But what could he do? A woman—even if the woman had been Paula Capperson—was dead. No one was going to make a fuss over the death of a woman who was practically invisible and very much disliked. Yet, Mayor White thought, Paula Capperson did, for better or worse, deserve justice—even if it meant that Mayfield would suffer a financial hit to the nose. "Well, at least I tried," he said in a defeated voice. "And you ladies make sure the good people of Mayfield know that."

Rhonda stood up. "Mayor," she said, feeling a liking for the worried man, "my sister and I will keep a low profile, okay? It's not like we're going to bust through the front doors of Green Valley Academy with flame throwers and grenades and begin accusing every student we see of murder. We are professionals."

Mayor White hadn't considered that Rita and Rhonda might be able to handle the case with kid gloves. Then, as he was considering the idea, a separate idea struck his worried mind. "Ladies, please come back to my office first thing in the morning and I will personally drive you up to the academy."

"That will be fine," Rita said. "We'll see you then." Rhonda nodded, and the two sisters left the office.

As soon as Rita and Rhonda were out of sight, Mayor White snatched up the phone sitting on his desk and called the hospital. "Yes, this is Mayor White...I need to speak to Dr. Varnell immediately." Mayor White popped a third piece of peppermint into his mouth and waited. A few minutes later, a man in his late sixties answered the call. "Jim...Barney..."

Dr. Jim Varnell sat down in a warm brown chair and took a sip of hot coffee. "It's a little too early to go ice fishing, Barney," he said, looking around a cozy break room filled with books. "Trying to get an early start won't work. I'm still going to win—"

"No, no, this isn't about the ice fishing contest," Mayor White fussed. "Jim, we go way back...way back...since grade school."

Jim crossed his right leg over his left knee. "Yes, we go way back, Barney. I was the best man at your wedding the day you married my sister."

"Then...I need you to do me a favor, Jim...for the sake of the town." Mayor White drew in a deep breath. "Paula Capperson is in the morgue, right?"

"Yes, her body arrived not long ago. Poor woman."

"I was told she was strangled?"

"That's how it appears." Jim nodded.

"Okay, Jim...I need you to write out a fake death certificate and then call Dave over at the funeral home and get him to...cremate the body."

Jim nearly spilled his coffee. "Barney, are you insane? What's going on?"

"Look," Mayor White snapped, "we have two very nosy women in town who might cause us to lose the academy. All because Ralph...that dummy...panicked and asked for outside help. If we can keep this matter local, then the state won't have to get involved and the two women who are biting at my ankles won't have a leg to stand on. All I need for you to do is say Paula Capperson killed herself, yeah, that's the way of it. Dave will cremate the body...and if Rita and Rhonda Knight still insist on being a problem, I can have them arrested. But as long as we have a body, we're the ones without a leg to stand on."

Jim put down his coffee. "Barney, are you drinking?"

"No, no, I'm not drinking!" Mayor White yelled. "Jim, you

know as well as I do if we lose the academy the entire town of Mayfield will sink under the snow before spring arrives. Now, I'm sorry that Paula Capperson is dead, but she's not worth a whole town suffering."

"Ralph informed me he has two outsiders helping him," Jim explained. "I don't see why that is causing you to act insane. How can two outsiders make us lose the academy?"

"Rita and Rhonda Knight believe someone at the academy killed Paula Capperson and plan to investigate...privately. And Jim, you better believe that if the state gets involved, the same idea might be thrown into the air."

Jim rubbed his chin and thought for a minute. He was earning very good money to be the official "Green Valley" medical doctor. The income he earned at the hospital was mere pennies compared to the money the academy filled his pockets with. Marla, his wife, enjoyed the money, the trips, the house, the fancy clothes, and other nice trimmings. If the academy closed up shop, he would be forced to move poor Marla back to Boston and begin working long hours again at a hospital he hated. "Barney, what you're asking is very risky."

"Look," Mayor White said, "I can handle Ralph, okay. Ralph told me that the only three people who saw Paula Capperson's body besides him were Rita and Rhonda Knight and Stan Hillside. Stan won't be a problem. He's one of us." Mayor White chewed on the peppermint in his mouth. "Dave can conduct the cremation."

"Barney, it's not that simple. There's procedures to follow and—"

"Jim, if we don't act, we could lose the academy," Mayor White snapped. "Now, we all know Paula Capperson has no family. We have to act fast."

"What if Paula Capperson does have family, Barney? Someone who pops up out of nowhere. How do we explain—"

"Oscar Frost was due to marry Paula Capperson," Mayor White explained. "That awful man came into my office a couple of weeks ago and dared to ask me to be his best man. I'm his only blood relative, and he told me Paula Capperson had no living family. Jim, Oscar is a moron, but why would he have lied about something like that?"

"You're risking a lot based off the word of Oscar Frost," Jim told Mayor White. "I…I just don't know."

"Well, you better know, because if the academy goes under, everyone in Mayfield is going to sink with it." Mayor White stood up. "Jim, I know I'm asking a lot, but it's for the good of the town—and the only way to make Rita and Rhonda Knight vanish. No body…no case."

"What if they claim otherwise?" Jim asked.

"That's where Ralph will come into play," Mayor White promised. "Ralph is going to change his tune, Jim, and show us how sorry he is for involving outsiders in a local matter."

"Don't get your feathers ruffled at Ralph," Jim insisted. "Barney, Ralph did what he thought was right. And in the current situation, I don't blame him for being unnerved. The man didn't even want to be sheriff, remember?"

"Yes, I remember."

"Ralph is a good man, Barney," Jim continued. "But if you press down too hard on him, he'll pack up shop and leave town. Can you imagine Ralph closing down his insurance business? Everyone will have to buy their coverage elsewhere at rates they won't be able to afford."

"I get it, Jim, I'll go easy on Ralph, okay?" Mayor White promised. He grabbed another piece of peppermint. "Can you get the job done?"

Jim looked down at his cup of coffee. "We can't risk losing the academy."

"No, we can't."

Jim grew silent for a minute and then said in a reluctant voice: "Okay, Barney, call Dave and explain the situation. If

Dave is willing to give us a green light, I'll write up the fake death certificate."

"Dave will play ball," Mayor White said in a relieved voice. "We've known Dave since grade school, too. I'll be in touch." Mayor White put down the phone and closed his eyes. "I'm sorry, Ms. Capperson, it's the only way," he said in a sad voice. He then called Restful Snow Funeral Home and spoke to an old friend. As he expected, the conversation ended in a green light being given. "Okay, Dave, I'm going to call Jim back. You get on over to the hospital and get the body and get the job done."

Mayor White hung up the phone and called Jim. Jim listened and then agreed, albeit reluctantly, to play ball. Paula Capperson was about to vanish from the face of the earth, leaving a killer at ease and two seasoned cops from out of town very angry.

chapter four

When Sheriff O'Neil showed up at the Snowdrift Inn a little past nine o'clock that evening, Rita and Rhonda both knew something was amiss. "Sheriff?" Rita said, noticing the man was wearing a plain gray coat over a pair of tan slacks instead of his sheriff's uniform.

"Ladies, may I come in?" Sheriff O'Neil asked in a quick voice. He tossed his head backward, studied the snow-soaked parking lot, focused on the lonely dark road lined with white trees covered with thick snow, and then looked back at Rita and Rhonda. "It's important that I speak with you."

Rita and Rhonda were both wearing warm robes. Rita's was blue and Rhonda's was pink. Allowing a man into their hotel room while dressed for bed didn't feel right. "Give us a minute," Rita replied as an icy wind grabbed at Sheriff O'Neil's face, "we need to get dressed." Rita closed the door. "This can't be good," she said in a quick voice. "Hurry and get dressed."

Rhonda threw on a gray dress with white stripes while Rita chose a dark green dress. "We better put on our shoes and make sure our guns are at arm's reach," Rhonda told Rita. Rita agreed. "Ready?" Rhonda asked.

"Ready," Rita said. She backed up to a bed covered with a warm green and brown quilt, sat down, and placed her gun under a white towel. Rhonda nodded and opened the hotel room door. "Come in, Sheriff."

Sheriff O'Neil studied the snowy parking lot once more. The SUV Rita and Rhonda had rented was the only patron visiting the parking lot. The SUV was cold and soaked with snow, showing that Rita and Rhonda had been at the hotel for at least two good hours. "Okay," he said as he stepped into the hotel room. Rhonda closed the door, eased over to a wooden writing desk, sat down, and placed her hand close to a towel resting on the desk.

"Sheriff, what brings you here?" Rita asked.

Sheriff O'Neil looked around the warm hotel room consumed with snowflake walls and a dark pine green rug. "Ladies, I'm scared," he said in a shaky, squeaky voice. "I'm...I don't want to be held responsible...I don't know what to do."

Rita shot a worried eye at her sister. "Sheriff, please tell us what's wrong."

Sheriff O'Neil shoved his hands into the pockets of his coat. "Paula Capperson's body has been cremated," he said in a sorrowful voice.

"Cremated?" Rita repeated in a shocked voice.

Sheriff O'Neil nodded. "Barney...uh, Mayor White... called me earlier and...he strong-armed me into agreeing with his plan. I should have said no...but...he made me feel responsible because I involved you two ladies in a local matter."

"Murder isn't a local matter," Rhonda said in an angry voice. "Oh, I could kick myself. I actually liked that little rat."

"Mayor White is a good man at heart," Sheriff O'Neil insisted. "He—" Before Sheriff O'Neil could finish his sentence, his cell phone began to ring in his front right coat pocket. "I better take the call," he said in an urgent voice, pulling out the black phone. "Yes, hello...what? Okay...okay...I'll drive to the hospital as quickly as I can."

"What's happening?" Rita demanded.

Sheriff O'Neil tossed his cell phone back into his coat pocket. "Haley Wellington just tried to kill herself," he told Rita in an upset voice. "Her mother found her passed out on her bed with an empty bottle of sleeping pills lying next to her. What in the world is going on?"

Rhonda jumped to her feet, threw Rita her coat, and then grabbed her gun. "We'll follow you, Sheriff," she said.

Sheriff O'Neil watched Rita and Rhonda put on their coats, conceal their guns, and then grab their purses. As upset and confused as he was, it felt good to have two honest—albeit retired—cops at his side. "You ladies can ride with me," he said. "I might be driving too fast to follow."

"Then let's move," Rhonda announced. She hurried out into the night snow with Rita, jogged to the sheriff's gray Jeep, and jumped inside. Rita followed. Sheriff O'Neil climbed into the driver's seat and got the Jeep moving. Twenty minutes later, he pulled up in front of the main entrance to a single-story brick building shaped like a fat square. "You ladies stay in the front lobby. I'll go to the ER and check on Haley and then come back and tell you what's happening."

"Deal," Rhonda said. Sheriff O'Neil zoomed out of the Jeep and aimed his legs at the front entrance.

"He's a decent man," Rita said. "He wants to do the right thing."

Rhonda bit down on her lip. "Yeah, well, Paula Capperson's body has been cremated, Sis. No body...no case. I'm not sure what the good sheriff wants us to do."

"Maybe this Haley Wellington girl will be able to help us?" Rita suggested.

Rhonda crawled out into the snow and locked eyes with a dark and snowy night. She grabbed the collar of her coat and tucked away from a cruel, icy wind. "Rita, can you believe what Sheriff O'Neil told us in the car, that Dr. Varnell wrote out a fake death certificate for Paula? He wrote that the cause of death was suicide."

Rita moved close to Rhonda. "The funeral home director, if questioned, will claim that Paula Capperson had a prearranged cremation already paid for," she added, speaking over the icy wind. "It wouldn't be hard to create false documents."

"Documents that no one in the world is interested in," Rhonda pointed out. "Paula was a loner. She has no family. Who cares if she's dead or alive? Even if we go to the state with Sheriff O'Neil and have him confess the truth, what will happen?"

"The killer will remain free while Mayor White and his friends are investigated. We would only be hurting people who broke the law in order to protect their town," Rita explained.

"Exactly." Rhonda nodded. "We're up a creek without a paddle."

"And freezing to death. Come on, let's get inside." Rita rushed Rhonda into a small front lobby lined with a hardwood floor and a row of green sitting chairs surrounded by white walls holding so-called artwork that made both women cringe. "Better," she said, feeling warm air begin to touch her face. "I forget how close we are to the Canadian border and how cold it is this far north."

Rhonda rubbed her hands together. "We forgot our gloves."

"I know," Rita moaned. She looked toward a set of double wooden doors. The doors opened up into a hallway that led to the ER. "Sheriff O'Neil might be a while," she said and sat down in one of the green chairs.

Rhonda blew on her hands and then joined her sister. "Paula Capperson is dead...now a young girl tries to kill herself. I think the two are connected."

"Me, too," Rita agreed. "How? That's the question."

Rhonda folded her arms. As she did, Oscar Frost walked through the main entrance. "Oh brother, what is he doing here?"

Oscar spotted Rita and Rhonda and walked over to them. "I have a police scanner," he announced in a proud voice. "I heard the call and thought I would stroll over to this medical hub and see what all the fuss is about."

"A young girl tried to kill herself," Rita snapped.

"A young girl, my lovely, who is the daughter of the local mayor's brother," Oscar explained in a curious tone. "The brother, mind you, is adopted, but still family, I suppose—at least to our dear mayor. I personally do not care for the sap."

Rita and Rhonda looked at each other. Oscar obviously was aware of a very vital piece of information. "Talk to us, jerk," Rhonda demanded.

"For a mere kiss." Oscar winked at Rhonda.

Rhonda yanked out her gun and pointed it at Oscar. "For a mere bullet, worm."

Oscar tossed his hands up in the air. "Alas, the Romeo and Juliet theme has arrived...parting is such sweet sorrow."

Rhonda rolled her eyes and put her gun away. "You're here for a reason. Spill the beans."

Oscar grinned. "Okay," he said in an excited voice that actually came out normal, "here's the deal." He plopped down beside Rita and rubbed his hands together. "I'm working on my first mystery novel. So far, my work has been lacking...shall we say...a certain flair. But now, oh, such excitement in this drab little town. My mind is very curious as to what data I might be able to steal in order to liven up a boring manuscript."

"I should have known," Rhonda said, feeling like she wanted to punch Oscar in the nose.

Oscar shrugged his shoulders. "Think of me what you will, but I have a book to write, and right now I'm at Deadville." Oscar leaned back. "Dear Paula is dead... strangled. Now Haley Wellington is having her stomach pumped. Why? And where is the killer? Something is amiss in Mayfield, and this man of words wants to find the missing snowflake."

"You have no conscience, you rat," Rhonda snapped at Oscar. "You're lucky I don't punch your lights out."

Rita held up a calming hand. "Oscar, can you tell us who Haley Wellington's parents are?"

"Sure," Oscar said. "Jackson Wellington is the local banker, and his darling wife is a sweet little old housewife who tends to the flower club and bake sales...but she burns her cakes. You didn't hear that from me."

"You seem to know a lot about people," Rita remarked, looking at Rhonda. "Doesn't he, Sis?"

Rhonda caught on to Rita's thought. "Why, yes, he does."

Oscar shrugged his shoulders. "I'm a man of words. It's my duty to be observant and to be aware of my surroundings, bland though they may be."

"If Mayfield is so boring, why not leave? Why not go to... oh, say...Los Angeles?" Rita asked.

"Oh no," Oscar laughed, "not Oscar Frost."

"Why not?" Rita pressed.

Oscar looked at Rita with suddenly serious eyes. "In Mayfield, I am unique. If I went to Los Angeles or New York, I would just be another freak in the crowd. Get it?"

"I guess," Rita said and eased Oscar back into the area she needed him. "So you know everyone in Mayfield?"

"I have eyes...I take walks," Oscar said in a careful voice.

"You mean you're a Peeping Tom," Rhonda corrected Oscar.

Oscar gave a casual shrug of the shoulder. "Call me what you may. A man of words has to understand those he chooses to paint with words."

"So you must know a lot about Haley Wellington's parents, right?" Rita asked, grateful that Rhonda was playing the bad guy which allowed her to manipulate Oscar into confessing vital information. Oscar was simply too stupid to know he was being played.

"Look, babe," Oscar said, patting Rita's hand, "Jackson and Lynn Wellington are about as interesting as a snail crossing a salt lick, okay? I mean, they're so clean they squeak. But," Oscar grinned, "little Miss Haley...oh, she's not so clean."

"What do you mean?" Rita asked, eyes wide.

"Oh, why bother with this jerk?" Rhonda said. "He's not going to give you a straight answer."

"Give him a chance, Sis," Rita snapped. She looked at Oscar. "Oscar, honey, what do you mean Haley isn't clean?"

Oscar liked being called "honey." He melted into Rita's beautiful eyes. "Haley attends the local high school, good-looking," he whispered. "But on the side, she sneaks up to the snooty school and holds hands with a rich boy. And at times," Oscar glanced around, "the rich boy leaves his web and ventures into town to see her."

"What's so strange about that?" Rhonda asked.

Oscar's grin widened. "The rich boy, babe—"

"Stop calling me babe or I'll sock you a good one," Rhonda promised Oscar.

Oscar held up his hands. "Let's not become Romeo and Juliet just yet," he teased and then moved forward. "The rich boy is the son of a very, very, very rich man and woman who reside in Switzerland. The man is a banker, and the woman is some kind of political face."

"So?" Rhonda asked.

"So," Oscar said in a delicious voice, "once he's done with

school, their son is set to marry the daughter of a very prominent loudmouth who sits high up in the European Union. If word got loose that the rich boy was holding hands with a local peasant...oh, how dreadful." Oscar threw his hands over his mouth and made a shocked face.

Rita studied every word that Oscar spoke. "Oscar, honey," she said, keeping up her act, "Paula Capperson told you all of this, didn't she?"

"Alas, brains and beauty," Oscar sighed.

Rita nodded. "Rhonda, maybe it isn't a coincidence that Haley Wellington was seeing the son of a prominent European banker."

"Oh, be still my beating heart," Oscar gasped, "your sweet words have tasted my mind."

"Oh, shut up," Rhonda snapped. She stood up and looked down at Rita. "Paula could have caught a scent of something that wasn't meant for her nose?" Rita nodded, and Rhonda continued. "I think we need to speak to Haley Wellington's boyfriend."

"First thing tomorrow," Rita agreed. She looked at Oscar and wondered what else the little runt knew. "Oscar, did Paula tell you anything else?"

"Oh," Oscar said in an excited voice, "Paula confessed many secrets to me. You see, on the outside Paula was a flat, boring canvas, but on the inside, she was a sneaky creature who liked to peek into the lives of people in order to write them down on paper. In other words, Paula was a nosy woman who kept tabs on all of her students." Oscar looked up at Rhonda. "As well as journals," he added and winked. "That's a freebie...babe."

Rhonda nearly punched Oscar but Rita stopped her. "Oscar, honey, where can we get some coffee?"

"The snack bar is not far away, my love," Oscar said and jumped to his feet. "How does my sweet darling prefer her coffee?"

Rita slowly stood up. "With company," she said and patted Oscar on his shoulder. "Rhonda, maybe you better go get some fresh air," she said in a voice that told Rhonda it was time to break into Paula's home and go treasure hunting.

"I guess I should before I cream this little runt," Rhonda said. She whipped around and stormed outside.

"Coffee?" Rita asked Oscar. Oscar beamed. "Lead the way."

"Okay," Rhonda whispered as she tucked her head down against the snow, "I hope you don't get mad at me for borrowing your Jeep, Sheriff."

Sheriff O'Neil, of course, wasn't even aware that Rhonda was taking his Jeep. He was standing over a beautiful young girl who had a tube down her throat.

Rhonda parked in front of Paula's house. The house was dark. A snow-soaked roof dripped with icy danger, landing in a spooky white yard trapped in a deep nightmare. "Okay, let's get inside," she whispered. She eased out of Sheriff O'Neil's Jeep and carefully journeyed around the dark house to the broken kitchen window. "I'll go through—" she began to whisper but stopped when her eyes spotted the kitchen window. It was open. Someone was in the house. Rhonda eased forward on silent legs and peered through the broken window. She spotted a flashlight beam racing around the interior of the kitchen. "Oh," she whispered. Hurrying behind the large tree resting in the side yard, she pulled out her gun and waited.

Minutes passed. Rhonda waited, shivering from top to bottom. Just when it seemed the intruder was never going to leave the house, the kitchen window suddenly slammed shut. Rhonda tensed up and waited. A few minutes later, the back door flung open and a dark shadow plunged outside on lightning-fast legs.

"Freeze!" Rhonda yelled and dashed off into the snow. The shadowy figure glanced over his shoulder, saw Rhonda running through the darkness, and picked up speed. Rhonda, running through ankle-deep snow, tried to keep pace, but, to her frustration, the intruder was making tracks running toward a snowy tree line. "Stop or I'll shoot!" Rhonda screamed. The shadowy figure ignored Rhonda, dived into the tree line, and vanished.

Rhonda gritted her teeth, bore down, and ran into the tree line. "Stupid..." she scolded herself. "I should have watched the back door." Rhonda stopped running and looked around, breathing hard white trails of smoke. All her eyes saw were dark trees covered with snow. The intruder was gone. "I can follow his tracks," Rhonda whispered. She carefully lowered her head, studied the snow, and began following a set of deep tracks. "Looks like a men's size ten...maybe an eleven..."

Rhonda followed the tracks, struggling to see through the darkness as she fought snow away from her face. She walked for a very long time, journeying north and drawing deeper into the woods. When she came to an icy stream, she groaned in frustration. "No," she muttered. She threw her head to the left, saw only darkness, and then looked to the right and saw nothing promising. "Oh," she fussed and focused on the stream. "I can't give up." Rhonda drew in a frozen breath and stepped into the ankle-deep water. "Cold...cold...so cold..." She winced and hurried across the shallow stream onto dry ground and immediately began searching the snow. "No prints...the intruder must have run up and down the stream and exited somewhere..." Rhonda raised her head up into the snow. "I better get back before this snow covers my own tracks and I get lost."

Rhonda hurried back across the stream, and with strained

eyes followed her tracks back to Paula's house. "Whew, for a minute I thought I was going to end up lost in the woods," she said in a relieved voice. "That would not have been good in this weather." She walked to the back door and carefully entered the kitchen with her gun at the ready. The kitchen was clear.

"Okay," Rhonda said to herself. She flipped on the kitchen light, locked the back door, and looked around. "Let's try and find out what the intruder was searching for." Rhonda kicked snow off her wet boots and began a slow, painful, methodical search. She ended up in a master bedroom that resembled a bedroom from the Victorian era.

"Paula had taste, I give her that," Rhonda said, and with a gentle respect began searching her bedroom. Coming up emptyhanded, she focused on the bedroom closet. "Ah," she said, spotting an open box resting on the closet floor. "What do we have here?" The box was empty. The word "Private" was neatly written on the side of the box with a green Sharpie.

"Great." Rhonda grabbed the box and walked back to the kitchen and called the hospital. "Yes, I need to speak to Rita Knight. Can you page her, please?" she told a woman manning the phones. A few minutes later, Rita came on the line. "Bad news, Sis."

"Tell me," Rita said, standing at a small nurses' station and staring at a room filled with a nervous sheriff, a relieved doctor, two scared parents, and a happy nurse.

"When I arrived at Paula's I encountered an intruder," Rhonda explained. She plopped down at the kitchen table and set the empty box down. "I gave chase, Rita, but the intruder outran me. He ran into the woods. I was able to follow his tracks but lost them when I came up on a stream. I barely found my way out back." Rhonda bent down and rubbed her frozen ankles. "I checked the house, Rita, and found an empty box in Paula's closet with the word 'Private' written on it. I think the contents inside the box were what the intruder was after."

Rita glanced to her right and saw Oscar standing at the entrance leading into the examining area. Dr. Varnell had kicked Oscar out of the examining area and Sheriff O'Neil had threatened him with arrest if he stepped one toe through the entrance door. "What are you thinking?" she asked Rhonda.

"Intruder had to be a teenager. No adult could take off through the snow like he did," Rhonda explained. "I'd say he was at least six foot. He was wearing all black, but I could see that the kid was pretty big...muscular." Rhonda continued to rub her ankles. "I threatened to shoot him, but he kept running. I had a clear shot at him for a few seconds, too."

"I think you encountered our killer."

"Yep." Rhonda agreed. "Looks like we're going to be making a trip up to Green Valley Academy tomorrow." Rhonda stopped rubbing her ankles. "What's the news on your end?"

"Haley Wellington is going to pull through," Rita said in a relieved voice. "Dr. Varnell said she got to the ER just in time." Rita locked her eyes on the examining room. "Sheriff O'Neil is in with her now."

Rhonda whispered a prayer for Haley. "I'm very happy to have some good news tonight."

Rita nodded. "I've got more news," she said. "Mayor White had Jackson Wellington take money out of Paula's account and send it to the funeral home earlier tonight. Jackson Wellington had the transfer backdated to ensure their false story would have concrete evidence to back it up."

Rhonda crinkled her nose. "Wow, that's a serious felony, right? Mighty risky thing for a banker to do," she remarked. "The Feds can easily audit a bank system."

"I was thinking the same thing." Rita nodded. "I met Mr. Wellington...briefly...and he doesn't seem like the type of man who would be willing to break the law unless he was forced to." Rita spotted a tall, thin man with a thick gray mustache standing over a sleeping, broken doll. "I think Mr. Wellington was acting on behalf of his daughter. But I don't think Mayor White or anyone else knew why until tonight."

"So Haley Wellington is the one who threw the brick through Paula's kitchen window with the threatening note? Why? Because Paula knew about her relationship with our killer? Possibly. But Haley Wellington isn't a killer...so what happens? Her boyfriend pays Paula a visit...maybe to talk at first...but then decides to go ahead and kill Paula just like the note threatened?"

"Paula must have known the killer because she opened the back door for him," Rita pointed out.

Rhonda looked around the fancy kitchen. "Haley's boyfriend kills Paula with a rope."

"Could be we were wrong earlier and the killer wasn't intending on kidnapping Paula?" Rita suggested. "Could be—"

"The killer wanted to strangle Paula outside and drag her body out into the snowy woods?" Rhonda finished for Rita.

"Only the killer can tell us," Rita said.

Rhonda rubbed her chin. "Haley finds out that Paula is dead...she freaks out...and then what?"

"She goes and tells her daddy the truth," Rita continued for her sister. "And before the hour passes, Mayor White sticks his nose into an already tragic situation and tells Haley's daddy that he has to manipulate Paula's bank records in order to save the town."

"Mr. Wellington, fearing for his daughter, agrees." Rhonda nodded. "But Haley...torn with guilt...maybe her daddy yelled at her...rushes to her bedroom—"

"While Mr. Wellington rushes to the bank."

"Haley, unable to bear the shame and guilt...does what?" Rhonda asked. "She calls her boyfriend and tells him goodbye. But then what? Does the boyfriend try to talk her out of it…or did he push the poor girl into taking the sleeping pills?" Rhonda bit down on her lip. "The kid broke into Paula's house to cover his own tracks, Sis. I doubt he cares that Haley Wellington almost died tonight. My guess is he might have threatened to kill Haley Wellington, and the poor girl—"

"Seeing no way out decides to kill herself," Rita finished for Rhonda. "We could be right, or we could be wrong, Sis. But right now, let's assume that we're right."

"Which means our next step is to visit a very ugly private academy that's hosting a killer."

"And when the situation allows, we need to talk to Haley Wellington," Rita added. She drew in a calm breath. "Rhonda, as it stands, Paula's death doesn't really need to be brought to the attention of any outside agency. Yes, we both know that certain men committed criminal acts tonight, but the intention was noble."

"What you're saying is that since Paula's body is gone, there's no need to cause trouble for this little town, right?"

"Yes," Rita admitted. "If we capture Paula's killer and try to connect him to Paula's death, we're going to cause more harm than good. However, if we can force the killer to come after us?"

"You mean you want us to become bait."

"There's no evidence that the kid you encountered tonight killed Paula. Paula's body is…cremated. That puts the town of Mayfield in the clear and settles the mayor down. However, that leaves the killer in the clear." Rita glanced at Oscar. Oscar gave her a finger wave. "We owe it to Paula to make sure her killer faces justice. But Rhonda, we have to draw the killer into town and away from the academy. We have to make the killer leave Mayfield."

Rhonda was surprised at her sister. "You really want to protect this little town, don't you?"

Rita sighed. "As much as I disagree with the criminal steps the mayor and his friends took tonight, I can also understand why, Rhonda. This isn't our town. But what if it was? What if our livelihood depended on one certain place?" Rita shook her head. "Paula Capperson didn't contribute to the welfare of Mayfield. She was a snotty, rude, antisocial woman...it pains me to speak of a dead woman that way." Rita shook her head again. "Is the death of one woman who wore ice on her shoulders worth a town falling?"

"No," Rhonda answered simply. "I've been struggling with that question ever since I left the hospital. The truth is...I can't really blame Mayor White for taking drastic actions tonight. The truth is, Sis, the law is the law...but sometimes the law has to fit the situation. Sometimes a cop has to step outside of all the red tape and just let folks do what they know is right."

"People matter," Rita said in a soft voice, looking toward the room Haley Wellington was resting in. "And Rhonda, because people matter, you and I are going to catch ourselves a killer, because if we don't—"

"The killer might try to finish Haley Wellington off," Rhonda finished for Rita.

"Yes," Rita said. "What began with Paula Capperson can spread into a wildfire. We have to get this killer out of town and have him focus entirely on us." Rita grew silent for a minute. "Rhonda," she finally spoke, "if the killer does harm Haley, everything these men worked for tonight, as criminal as it was, will fall apart. We have an innocent girl to protect, and an entire town."

"Hey, you know me," Rhonda said, feeling her frozen ankles whining, "I don't leave the game until the last inning. Besides, at least I'm not falling out of the back of a speeding truck," she joked.

"And at least I'm not trying to be thrown into a dark hole in some old mining tunnel," Rita tried to joke back. Then Billy suddenly came into her mind. "Oh no, Billy is on his way up, Rhonda. I better call him and have him cancel the trip."

Rhonda stood up. "I'm on my way back to the hospital," she informed Rita in a tired voice. "I'll secure the house and be at your location in about half an hour or so. In the meantime, yes, call Billy and tell him to go back home."

"What choice do I have?" Rita asked. "I'll see you in a bit." Rita ended the call and then dialed Billy's cell phone number. Billy picked up on the third ring. "Were you asleep?"

Billy sat up on a lumpy bed and rubbed his eyes. "I reckon I was," he admitted in a sleepy voice. I just laid down to rest my eyes for a second...reckon I dozed off. Why, I'm still in my overalls and got my boots on." Billy spotted Chester lying at the foot of the bed. "Reckon Chester and me are plum pooped."

Rita felt bad for waking Billy up. "Where are you?"

"Oh, somewhere, I guess." Billy yawned. "I pulled off onto this little exit and found me a motel called the Guitar Inn. Can't say this place is anything fancy, but what do you expect for thirty-five dollars a night? Sure beats them chain places that charge a person an arm and a leg."

Rita pictured Billy sitting in a cheap hotel in the middle of nowhere next to a single gas station and a rundown garage. Only Billy. "Billy...I...hate to disturb you—"

"Not at all."

Rita closed her eyes and saw Billy's sweet face appear. "Billy, Rhonda and I are kinda up to our neck in...trouble and...you might want to turn around and go back home."

Billy stood up. "Trouble?" he asked in an alarmed voice. "You tell Billy what kind of trouble is chasing you, you hear?"

Rita felt a gentle smile touch her lips but then frowned just as quickly. "Murder, Billy," she whispered. "Rhonda and I are after a killer, and it looks like the chase is going to be very difficult."

Billy walked to the window, pulled back a brown curtain,

and looked out into a dark, cold night. "Billy ain't going back home," he informed Rita. "Now, I may not be all brains, but I do have a backbone and I stand by folks I care about."

Rita sighed. Billy was her hero. But what if he ended up dead?

Far away from Billy, a very angry killer burst into a room and began reading through Paula's private journals.

chapter five

Rita stopped at the bottom of a twisty, snowy road. "The road hasn't been plowed," she told Rhonda in a concerned voice. "I don't think this SUV will be able to make the climb."

Rhonda stuck her gloved hands to the hot air flooding out of the front vents. "No way this SUV is going to climb that hill," she agreed. "Looks like we're walking."

"Ugh, I thought you'd say that." Rita shoved the SUV into park. "The academy has canceled all classes for the remainder of the week in honor of Paula. All students have been asked to use the week to study for their final exams before Thanksgiving break." Rita studied the snowy road. "Having the students remaining on the property is a real break, but pretending to be state health inspectors claiming Paula was sick before she died in order to get inside...I don't know, that's risky, Rhonda."

"We're going to insist that Paula was carrying a very ugly virus and that we need to check each student and staff member. It'll work," Rhonda insisted. "It sure beats sneaking around like criminals. You heard Sheriff O'Neil, he said the headmaster, this Mr. Tulley, has locked down the grounds for the entire week. We can't wait that long, Sis."

"I know," Rita agreed in a sleepy voice. She grabbed a silver travel mug and took a sip of hot, fresh coffee. "The killer saw you, Rhonda. That's my worry."

"It was really dark, Rita. I could only make out the outward features on the punk who ran from me. I'm sure he didn't stand around and stare at my face. Besides, the wind was really up. Maybe he didn't even hear me when I yelled at him to stop running."

"Maybe he did."

"Well, that's a chance we're going to have to take," Rhonda said in a serious voice. "We have to set the bait."

Rita knew her sister was right. She put down the travel mug and tightened her coat. "Okay," she said, mentally preparing for a cold walk, "let's move."

Rhonda nodded, secured the pink ski cap she was wearing, made sure Rita's gray ski cap was good, and crawled out into the heavy snow. Rita turned off the SUV and joined her sister. "My, the snow is really coming down...and the wind..." Rhonda said, tucking her chin down against the howling winds.

Rita folded her arms together and nodded at the snowy road. "We have a long walk ahead of us. Sheriff O'Neil said this road climbs up for almost a mile. We better get moving."

Rhonda nodded, checked her gun, and got her legs moving through the deep snow. "Forget needing a treadmill," she said as her legs began climbing the road, "this climb alone will burn off a year's worth of calories."

Rita stepped off the public road and placed her own feet into knee-deep snow that was covering the private road leading up to the academy. "This walk isn't going to be easy," she complained, taking one difficult step after another.

Rhonda stopped walking and looked to her left and then to her right. All she saw were white, snow-covered trees hiding vast amounts of wild country. "A person can really get lost out here," she said, breathing white trails of smoke from her mouth. "The punk I was chasing last night sure seemed to know his way around...which makes me wonder..."

"Wonder what?" Rita asked.

"The stream I encountered," Rhonda explained. "I wonder if it's close by."

"Rhonda, we don't have time—"

"No, what I mean is..." Rhonda bit down on her lower lip. "Sis, listen, the kid I tried to chase down might or might not get spooked when we reach the academy. I think maybe we need to make a quick change in plans."

"Such as?" Rita asked, feeling moist, thick snowflakes flying into her face.

"Let me stay behind and look around some," Rhonda explained. "I'll see if I can locate the stream...or any escape route our killer might try to take if he gets spooked and tries to run. Could be he has a hidden snowmobile around here someplace or a pair of skis. Who knows?"

"How about I do that and you pretend to be the state health inspector?" Rita offered. "Besides, your eyes will lock on the killer quicker than mine since you've physically seen him."

Rhonda wiped snow away from her eyes. "There's a chance the punk might run and then there's a chance he might actually play dumb. But...either way, I do think it's smart if one of us hangs out in this snow and has a good look around." Rhonda looked at Rita. "We'll walk to the top of the road together and then split up. You can take the outside and I guess I'll play nurse since it was my idea."

"Okay then, what are we waiting for?" Rhonda got her legs moving, and, like a beautiful ice princess, began climbing the road.

"Rita?" Rhonda asked, keeping her head tucked down against the wind.

"Yes?"

"Our bakery was a success this year, wasn't it?" Rhonda said.

"It certainly was. We have Erma to thank for that," Rita said.

Rhonda focused on the hard climb. "And...Clovedale Falls, it's a real nice town, isn't it?" she said in a voice that made Rita look sideways at her.

"Yes, Clovedale Falls is a very nice town, Rhonda. Why?" Rita asked curiously, barely making her voice heard over the howling winds.

Rhonda grew silent for a couple of minutes as she worked through the deep snow. "Leaving our bakery to our children someday would be nice."

"Rhonda, we don't have any children," Rita stated in a sad voice. She tucked her head low and pushed forward. Walking through the knee-deep snow was proving to be a real task.

"Exactly," Rhonda replied. "Rita, you and I are childless... we're not married..." Rhonda glanced sideways at her frozen sister. "Every day that passes we grow older...and...still no husband or children. And to be honest, I'm not sure my body can handle being pregnant at this age. We're still closer to forty than we are fifty, but that's going to change...and...even if it didn't...having a baby at our age can be very difficult."

"Yes, I suppose it can." Rita nodded, feeling Rhonda's sadness lean over and touch her.

"And each day that passes," Rhonda continued as she dug one foot out of the snow and planted it forward, "is a day that we're still not married. No husband...no children." Rhonda sighed. "I want a family, Rita...a beautiful, traditional family. I want to bake cookies and fix school lunches for my kids and kiss my husband goodbye when he leaves for work. I want... the whole Donna Reed and Father Knows Best package. Instead, I'm stuck out here in this snow playing cop again."

"We can turn around, leave Mayfield and fly back home?"

"I would never be able to forgive myself if I did," Rhonda

told her sister. "You saw Haley Wellington this morning at the hospital. That girl is blessed to be alive."

"I just wish she would have talked to us," Rita remarked.

"The fear in that girl's eyes told us all we needed to know."

"Yes, that's true," Rita said and dared to look up. The snowy, twisting road grinned at her. "Haley's boyfriend threatened her, that was clear to see. The poor girl...caught between her daddy's anger and her boyfriend's threat—"

"Not to mention the guilt she was feeling over Paula's murder."

"Her little emotions just couldn't deal with the nightmare she was trapped in," Rita finished. "I—" Rita stopped speaking when she heard someone yell out her name. She turned around and saw Oscar waving at her.

"Wait up!" Oscar yelled, struggling through the deep snow. "My love, your Romeo has arrived!"

"Are you *kidding* me?" Rita moaned.

"Let's shoot the little runt and bury his body under the snow," Rhonda begged. "One bullet...POW!" Rhonda formed her hand into a gun and fired a make-believe bullet at the pesky little man.

"Don't tempt me," Rita told Rhonda as she watched Oscar climb through the snow like a sad little kid forcing his body through a room full of thick cotton candy.

"My love...oh, I have found thee," Oscar called out, breathing so hard he could barely speak.

"He's a sad person who just wants attention," Rita told Rhonda. "Pity him and...humor him, okay?"

Rhonda fired a second make-believe bullet at Oscar. "Too bad I missed." She grinned.

Oscar watched Rhonda lower her hand and rolled his eyes. "I have feelings, you know!" he yelled as he finally reached Rita.

"You do?" Rhonda asked in a shocked voice. "Golly, Mr.

Frost, who would have known?" Rhonda rolled her eyes. "Get lost."

"Never," Oscar cried out and grabbed Rita's hand. You are Rita, right?" he asked and quickly studied Rita's face and then her hair. "Yes...you were wearing the gray ski cap earlier."

"Oscar," Rita said, feeling sorry for the guy, "what are you doing here?" Rita wanted to be angry, but for some reason the disgust she originally felt for Oscar had transformed into simple pity.

"I have come to protect thee, my love," Oscar said in a proud voice. "You and your...other half...are seeking a killer. I must ensure that you are protected against the unknown dangers lurking up this road."

Rhonda rolled her eyes again. "If you don't get caught in a snowdrift first," she said and let out a tired laugh. "You couldn't protect a tree from a squirrel, you little runt."

Oscar frowned. "I know you despise me," he said in a voice that came out serious and human rather than silly and eccentric. "I know you believe I'm a soulless man because I'm not showing any remorse over Paula's murder. But the truth is, I didn't love Paula and she didn't love me. We were two lonely people who agreed to become lifelong companions. Am I sorry she's dead? Yes. But what am I supposed to do? Sit around and cry all day?" Oscar let go of Rita's hand. "Look, girls, I know I'm a loser, okay? I know what the world thinks of me. I've experienced hatred and rejection all of my life, beginning with my parents." Oscar looked around at the snow. "Years ago I made a choice to be as eccentric and...and insane as possible... to become a disease in the eyes of the people I once worked so hard to impress. Why? Because no matter how hard I tried to be accepted I was constantly rejected. Women laughed at me... guys bullied me...family members mocked me. So I quit trying and became the exact opposite. And you know what?"

"What?" Rhonda asked.

"I feel free," Oscar announced and held his hands up in the air. "I don't care about people and people don't care about me. I can be as silly and eccentric as I want to be and it doesn't matter. Why? Because even if I acted like a perfect gentleman, the world would still reject me. So I act exactly how I want. But," Oscar added, still serious, "deep down, ladies, I still have a heart. I'm sorry Haley Wellington tried to kill herself. She's a sweet kid who got mixed up with a really bad guy. I'm sorry Paula is dead. She was a strange lady but okay on the inside." Oscar looked up at Rita. "I just don't see any sense in wasting what time I have on this earth trying to please others anymore. I have the right to be happy, too, you know."

"But you're not happy," Rita told Oscar. "I can look into your face and tell you're just acting. Everyone can."

"The face can hide a lot," Oscar told Rita. "Better to put on the face of an actor than to show the pain underneath." Oscar looked at Rhonda. "You want to know the real reason why I came here today?"

"Sure," Rhonda said.

"Paula's journals," Oscar said in a careful voice. "The shadow who broke into Paula's home didn't get the journal he was after. No sir."

Rita and Rhonda looked at each other. "And why not?" Rita asked over the howling winds.

"Because I have the journal." Oscar grinned. "I've read through all of Paula's journals and yesterday it occurred to me that it might be useful to hide a certain one. I went back to Paula's house after her body was taken away and found the journal." Oscar folded his arms. "Paula was very fond of sneaking into the records room and peeking into her students' private files. She was also fond of hacking into private accounts. You see, Paula wasn't as innocent as she looked.

Sure, she might not have been very attractive, but her brain was very clever."

Rita looked at Rhonda again. "Rhonda—"

"I know what you're thinking," Rhonda told Rita. "We need to alter our game plan again."

"Game plan?" Oscar asked.

"We'll explain later," Rita told Oscar. She looked up the twisting road. "Okay, Rhonda, we'll still go with your plan for now. But if you encounter the killer, use the new bait, okay?"

Rhonda nodded. "Our new bait is sure better than claiming we had an eyewitness to the murder."

"You do?" Oscar asked in a shocked voice.

"No...no," Rhonda said in an annoyed voice. "If we encountered the killer...if I encounter the killer...I was going to tell him there was an eyewitness to the murder and demand money and insist he meet me outside of Mayfield."

"Our goal is to draw the killer away from Mayfield, Oscar," Rita explained.

"By blackmailing him?" Oscar asked. "Oh, you two are tricky."

Rhonda rolled her eyes. "There's a chance the killer might not take the bait. But now that you have the journal he was looking for—"

"A journal I'm not handing over to anyone," Oscar quickly pointed out. "Not until," he said and smiled at Rita and then tossed a thumb at Rhonda, "not until your sister kisses me right on the lips. And I mean a real kiss...not just a peck. I want her to melt the snow."

"What?" Rhonda gasped. "Why, you little twerp...I wouldn't kiss you—"

"Bye-bye, journal," Oscar promised.

Rita looked at Rhonda. "We need that journal, Sis."

Oscar grinned. "Pucker up, babe."

"Pucker this," Rhonda said and slugged Oscar in the

stomach. "Rita, I'll go with my original plan, thank you very much."

Oscar dropped down onto his knees, grabbed his stomach, and began coughing. "Wow...what a woman..." He coughed. "But...no kiss...no journal. And before you...go traipsing up to the academy, there's something in the journal you need to know...something that will really help you."

"What?" Rhonda demanded.

Oscar rubbed his stomach and leered up at them. Rita and Rhonda looked at each other and rolled their eyes. It was time for Rhonda to pucker up.

Rhonda wanted to scald her lips. She felt like vomiting. "I'm going to demolish that little runt."

"What is that?" Mr. Edwin Tulley asked. He stopped walking down a long hallway lined with large stained-glass windows and looked at the beautiful woman standing next to him. "What did you say, Ms. Knight?"

"Oh, I said..." Rhonda glanced down at the very expensive grayish-black tile floor that cost more money than she would ever see in a lifetime. "I said...I was admiring the beauty of this building." Mr. Tulley reminded Rhonda of Robin Leach from the *Lifestyles of the Rich and Famous*. The man was wearing a crisp gray suit that cried of money. The suit matched his snotty face.

"This...building is a monstrosity," Mr. Tulley scowled. "The original structure was built by a brilliant Russian architect in 1878." Mr. Tulley looked at Rhonda. "The original structure had wood cut from the deepest German forest and stone cut from the cliffs of Norway. The...building...that stands now is a pathetic heap of junk."

"Uh...well, it seems very nice." Rhonda forced a fake smile to her face. "The tile floor is beautiful."

"The tile is cheap junk from France." Mr. Tulley glowered.

"Really?" Rhonda asked in a shocked voice. "It looks very expensive."

"To a common peasant, yes," Mr. Tulley explained in his snotty voice, "but to a man of my stature…no."

Rhonda fought the urge to roll her eyes. Edwin Tulley was nearly as bad as Oscar Frost in her view. "Mr. Tulley, I'm not here to admire the handiwork. Ms. Capperson was infected with a serious virus. I need to interview each of her students. If I spot any of them exhibiting symptoms, I will send them into town to see Dr. Varnell right away…without panic, of course."

Mr. Tulley made a sour face. "Ms. Capperson was a horrid woman," he announced. "I would have gratefully terminated the woman and paid her unemployment and faced any lawsuit she might have brought against the academy, but certain parents seemed to favor the woman. Why? I have never been able to figure out that riddle." Mr. Tulley lowered his voice. "I caught Ms. Capperson sneaking through private files on several occasions. When I replaced the lock on the file room door, I was informed by our computer team that certain violations had been conducted. Our computer team traced the violations to Ms. Capperson's laptop."

"Oh? Why didn't you fire her? You surely had the grounds to do so."

Mr. Tulley glanced around. "I was preparing to terminate the woman," he confessed in an even lower voice. "I was preparing to contact the parents and inform them of Ms. Capperson's violations. But then I received a call last night from Sheriff O'Neil. He informed me the horrid woman had killed herself." Mr. Tulley looked at Rhonda with careful eyes. "Ms. Knight, I am an educator. I am not a stupid man."

Rhonda studied Mr. Tulley's eyes. "You mean you don't believe Sheriff O'Neil?"

"I believe Ms. Capperson was murdered and I told Sheriff

O'Neil that very thing," Mr. Tulley confessed. "Ms. Capperson showed no strange behavior around me other than being a person who violated every privacy act in the book. No one single student seemed offended by her." Mr. Tulley shook his head. "I can't exactly pinpoint what I'm trying to say, but...I feel the woman was murdered. I fear she came across certain information that she shouldn't have."

"Oh?" Rhonda asked, playing dumb.

"Yes," Mr. Tulley whispered. "Ms. Knight, the children of very powerful people attend this academy. If Ms. Capperson stepped on some toes...well..." Mr. Tulley cleared his throat. "I spoke my piece. I've done so because if anything should happen to me, at least I have two witnesses who can possibly bring justice to my death."

Rhonda frowned. "Are you afraid someone might harm you?" she asked Mr. Tulley.

Mr. Tulley glanced around. "Whoever killed Ms. Capperson might hold me personally responsible," he confessed in an uneasy voice. "After all, I allowed Ms. Capperson to violate the rules without contacting any of the parents for over a year. Of course, I hid her violations because I feared the parents who favored her would refuse my request to terminate her. However..."

"However what?" Rhonda asked, not needing to pretend to seem curious. Was Mr. Tulley, the snotty headmaster, actually going to release helpful information—hidden information? Boy, what a morning.

"There is one parent who was lobbying for Ms. Capperson to be terminated."

"Really?"

Mr. Tulley looked around and gently walked Rhonda into a large, empty classroom. "Yes," he said in a careful voice. "Mrs. Angela Ryeberry."

"Am I supposed to recognize that name?"

Mr. Tulley looked at Rhonda as if the woman were insane.

"Mrs. Angela Ryeberry is the wife of Kent Ryeberry, a very wealthy European banker. She basically controls this academy."

"Oh...well, good for her," Rhonda said, still pretending to play dumb. "Is this the classroom I will be using?"

Mr. Tulley couldn't believe his ears. "Ms. Knight, are you mad?" he asked. "Angela Ryeberry has the power...or should I say, her husband's money has the power...to make any person suddenly...vanish." Mr. Tulley walked over to a large square window and looked out at a set of snowy woods. "Mrs. Ryeberry wasn't fond of Ms. Capperson. She claimed Ms. Capperson was too harsh on her son."

Rhonda saw an opening. "What is Mrs. Ryeberry's son's name?" she asked.

"Thorn Ryeberry," Mr. Tulley replied, keeping his back turned to Rhonda. If he was going to be killed...well, someone was going to know the truth. Of course, there was the grand possibility that his life would be spared and that his title as headmaster would survive for years to come. After all, Ms. Capperson was dead, the problem of her violations seemed to be solved, and he was still alive. Why create a bigger mess of things?

"Thorn Ryeberry is a dreadful student," Mr. Tulley went on. "As much as I detested Ms. Capperson, I could understand why she was so harsh with Thorn, and so did the other parents. Some of the parents convinced Mrs. Ryeberry to leave Ms. Capperson alone and even threatened to pull their children out of this academy if she objected to their request. That was a few months ago."

Rhonda eased close to the window. "There's always a troubled student in the batch, Mr. Tulley, and one or two unhappy parents around."

Mr. Tulley turned and looked into Rhonda's beautiful face. Beautiful women were a rarity at the Green Valley Academy. "Ms. Knight, there is a difference between a regular public school student who throws paper balls at the blackboard and a wealthy student who has power under his heels."

"I suppose," Rhonda said with a shrug. "Mr. Tulley, I really need to focus on interviewing the students."

Mr. Tulley shook his head. "You're as blind as the rest of them. You have no idea of the power some of my students hold."

Rhonda saw that she had Mr. Tulley completely where she wanted him. "Okay, so a few wealthy kids go here, so what? Mr. Tulley, this is a very expensive academy to attend. Tuition is seventy-five thousand dollars a year, after all. At least that's what I heard." Rhonda looked out the window at the snowy day. "But," she added, "I guess money doesn't replace a mother's instinct. If a teacher was being harsh on my child, I would want her replaced, too. I suppose you can't blame Mrs. Ryeberry for being upset with Ms. Capperson."

Mr. Tulley glanced at the closed door. "Ms. Knight, it was no secret that Mrs. Ryeberry was lobbying to have Ms. Capperson terminated. I...personally know Ms. Capperson was breaking into the students' files in order to gain information that would secure her teaching position. As much as it bothers me to admit this, Ms. Capperson was not a stupid woman." Mr. Tulley looked at the closed door again. "In the last months before her death, the horrid woman broke into the computer system on several occasions and looked into Thorn Ryeberry's private file. She continued her mission even after Mrs. Ryeberry was forced to stand down by some of the parents."

"I wonder why."

Mr. Tulley reached into his side pocket and pulled out a cigarette. "Mind?" Rhonda shook her head no. "Ms. Knight," he said as he lit the cigarette with a fancy silver lighter, "as I mentioned before, Thorn Ryeberry is a very problematic student. He's constantly bullying other students and breaking the rules."

"The rules?" Rhonda asked as cigarette smoke floated in front of her nose. She quickly slapped the smoke away.

"One rule in particular," Mr. Tulley pointed out and took a draw from his cigarette.

"What rule is that?"

"The rule that the parents insist their children follow," Mr. Tulley said. "No student from Green Valley Academy may date a local girl."

"What? Why?"

"Because, Ms. Knight," Mr. Tulley pointed out as he slowly exhaled a trail of smoke, "many students who attend Green Valley Academy are either willing or unwilling participants in prearranged marriages; Thorn Ryeberry is one of them. I've had to mark Thorn Ryeberry's personal file many times with black marks he earned by dating a local girl. The black marks were reported to his parents."

"That's...something," Rhonda said and shrugged her shoulder. "I guess?"

"Ms. Knight, you don't understand how important these prearranged marriages are," Mr. Tulley explained. "Many of the students who attend Green Valley Academy are being groomed to become the spouses of people who swim in power, politics, and money." Mr. Tulley worked on his cigarette. "You may or may not understand what I'm about to confess," he said, "but the parents who send their children to Green Valley Academy, regardless of their money and power, can very easily be marked an outcast if they fail to marry their child into a respectable family. It's all about reputation, status, power, money, and politics, Ms. Knight."

Rhonda began forming a theory in her mind. "Well, I really need to begin evaluating Ms. Capperson's students," she said. "I think I'll begin with Thorn Ryeberry since he seems to be problematic. I like to get the worst out of the way. I'm sure you understand."

Mr. Tulley opened the window, tossed out his cigarette,

popped a mint into his mouth, and looked at Rhonda. "If only you understood," he said in a disgusted voice. "I assumed a medical examiner like yourself would have some understanding. I was wrong. Now, if you will excuse me, I'll go get Thorn Ryeberry and send him your way."

Rhonda watched Mr. Tulley leave the empty room in a huff. She stepped close to the window, leaving her coat on, and looked out into the snow. "Rita, that stuffy snot just helped us out," she whispered. "I'll stick to the plan and see if I can get our killer to run, but if I fail, I think I have a surefire way to make our killer obey." Rhonda turned away from the window and waited. A few minutes later, a tall seventeen-year-old punk who resembled a powerful, angry Russian stepped into the classroom wearing a blue and gray school uniform. "Thorn Ryeberry?" Rhonda asked, hoping the killer wouldn't recognize her voice.

Thorn stared at Rhonda with careful eyes. He didn't recognize Rhonda or the voice she spoke with. "Mr. Tulley told me Ms. Capperson might have been sick?" he asked.

"Yes," Rhonda said, forcing her voice to sound professional.

Thorn's thoughts were on the missing journal and the stranger he had encountered at Paula's home the night before. The stranger, he thought, could have been Haley Wellington's old man. Thorn didn't know. All he knew was that Haley had run her mouth. He wasn't aware that Haley had tried to kill herself. However, Thorn was hoping the threat he made to the scared girl was enough to make her leave town. If Haley was stupid enough to stay, then she would have to die. "I don't feel sick."

Rhonda studied Thorn's face and then checked his build. Yeah, Thorn was the punk who had broken into Paula's home. "Ms. Capperson was a very close friend," she told Thorn, keeping her voice calm. "I was monitoring her illness. It wasn't until recently that I found out her illness could have become contagious." Rhonda stared at Thorn. "I'm very sad my friend is dead."

"I heard the lady killed herself," Thorn said in a cold voice.

"That's what I was told, too." Rhonda nodded and then carefully pulled out some bait and tossed it at Thorn. "Ms. Capperson was very concerned with her job here at the Green Valley Academy," she told Thorn, deciding to use the words Mr. Tulley had spoken to her advantage before grabbing onto the information Oscar had traded her for a kiss...the little runt. "Ms. Capperson told me there was a certain parent who was trying to get her fired. I begged her not to get upset because she was ill, but Paula kept insisting that she was being targeted." Rhonda shook her head. "The poor woman was frantic."

Thorn stared at Rhonda with eyes that would never gain a conscience. Even though he was only seventeen, his heart had already transformed into a hideous monster that would never understand the beauty of light and truth. "The woman was a horrible teacher. She was always riding my case. She should have been fired years ago."

Rhonda sighed. "I'm not her judge, young man. However, I will admit it was wrong for her to keep journals on her students and..." Rhonda paused. "Oh dear, did I just say that? I'm sorry. Please forget what I just said." Rhonda motioned for Thorn to step closer to her. "I need to examine you, please."

"What do mean Ms. Capperson kept journals?" Thorn snapped in a hard voice. What did the strange woman standing in the empty classroom know about the journals Paula had been keeping? He wanted answers. His mother wanted answers.

Rhonda sighed again. "I told Ms. Capperson that she was breaking the rules. I warned her that she risked losing her job if she continued to break the rules. But Paula...uh, Ms.

Capperson insisted that she was gathering information on her students in order to protect her job. Oh, it was a very ugly mess. But now the poor dear is dead. I suppose the stress of it all finally got to her. She wasn't well to begin with." Rhonda looked at the window. It was time to kick it into high gear. "I wish the poor woman wouldn't have involved me, but what are friends for?"

"Involved you?" Thorn asked. He stepped closer to Rhonda.

Rhonda turned her head and looked at Thorn. She played innocent. "I'm afraid the poor woman sent me one of the journals she was keeping on a certain student. I was going to return it to Mr. Tulley, your headmaster, but I left home in haste this morning and forgot all about it."

Thorn felt his heart begin to kick in his chest. The old bat had sent the strange chick standing in front of him the missing journal. "Where do you live?" he asked, trying to sound cool.

"In Mayfield." Rhonda smiled. "But I'm leaving for Georgia tonight. I have family there and, well, after losing my close friend, I need some breathing room. I'll be staying at my cousin Billy's farm in a town called Clovedale Falls." Rhonda pointed at Thorn. "But first I must make sure none of the students who came into contact with Ms. Capperson are ill."

Thorn nodded, let Rhonda examine him, and then left the classroom. "Okay, chick," he whispered under his breath, "you're going to die...but not here. Too many deaths in one place will look wrong. I'll follow you to Georgia, wherever that is." Thorn hurried back to his dorm room and began to throw some clothes and a deadly hunting knife into an expensive black leather suitcase. "I'll handle Haley and her old man when I get back. First, I have a journal to find."

chapter six

"Are you sure he took the bait?" Rita asked, blowing on her frozen hands.

"Oh, by the expression on the punk's face, I'm pretty sure he took the bait," Rhonda promised in a confident voice. "Now, let's get back to town, pack, and get back to Clovedale Falls. We have a skunk to catch."

Rita put her SUV into drive and drove away into a hard falling snow. Oscar followed closely behind in a rundown truck. "Oscar and I located the stream," she told Rhonda. "That's about all we did. It's so cold outside...I nearly froze in half."

As Rita drove away with Oscar on her tail, Thorn stepped out from behind a tree. "What is this?" he asked himself in a furious voice. "Two of them? And what was the stupid little man who was supposed to marry Capperson doing with them?" Thorn looked around. It was a good thing he had followed Rhonda back down the road. "This is a set-up...it has to be," he growled. "And I almost fell for it." Thorn punched the tree he was standing beside with an angry fist. Snow toppled off the tree and struck his face. "Mother, I'll do your dirty work, but you're going to owe me. Besides, this is all your fault. If you would have left the old bat alone like I asked she wouldn't have started stealing information. And you're the one who had that loser Tulley watch every move I made. If he hadn't marked my files with those black marks everything would be good. But that idiot had to black mark me every time I was seen with Haley." Thorn narrowed his eyes. "You owe me big time, Mother Dearest."

Thorn slithered back to his dorm, grabbed a pair of skis, and broke back into the snow. "I think I'll pay Haley a visit," he said and moved off into the snow using a private trail that ended up close to the back of a gingerbread-style neighborhood that was located only two blocks from Haley's house. When Thorn reached the end of the trail, he kicked off his skis, checked the black ski coat he was wearing to make sure he looked cool, checked his slick blond hair, and then moved out of the woods and began walking toward Haley's house. The walk was cold but easy. However, finding Haley's house empty was not easy. Thorn decided to climb up the tree sitting outside of Haley's bedroom window and look inside. The bedroom was dark and shadowy. "Did she leave town?" he asked in a hopeful voice as he skidded back down the tree. As he did, Old Man Walker came strolling by with his poodle on a leash. "Hey!" Thorn called out to the man. "Did the people living here leave town?"

Old Man Walker, a retired veterinarian, was too cold and far too grumpy to stop and talk. He looked at Thorn, saw a handsome young man, assumed he was one of Haley's boyfriends, and yelled in an irritated voice: "What are you, stupid? Haley tried to kill herself last night, boy. She's at the hospital recovering. Get a brain!"

Thorn watched Old Man Walker stroll away. He could have kicked the old man into the snow but didn't. Instead, he turned and aimed his body toward the hospital. The words "tried" and "at the hospital recovering" rang through his mind like loud bells exploding in a bell tower. "I better go stake out the hospital," he said in an urgent voice. He broke into a steady jog that was nothing for a healthy seventeen-year-old to accomplish. Twenty minutes later, he arrived at the hospital and ducked behind a parked truck just in time to see Rita and Rhonda pull up in front of the main entrance. Unfortunately, neither Rita nor Rhonda spotted Thorn. Poor Oscar, who pulled up behind Rita, didn't spot Thorn, either. Thorn crouched down and watched the twin sisters walk into the hospital, waiting until Oscar hurried after them before making his move.

Feeling like James Bond, Thorn slithered into the hospital. He walked up to a wooden desk manned by an old woman wearing a pink dress. "I'm here to see Haley Wellington, ma'am," he said in a voice that sounded polite and caring. The old woman smiled and made a call. Thorn waited.

"I'm sorry," the old woman told Thorn, "Haley Wellington was flown to the state capital early this morning. She is no longer a patient here."

Thorn felt anger strike his chest. Then an idea replaced his anger. He quickly let out a cough. "That's okay," he said, "I'll catch her later. Is it...okay if I sit down for a while? I don't feel so hot, you know?"

"Of course, dear," the old woman told Thorn in a worried voice. "Can I get you some water?"

"No...I'll be okay...maybe?" Thorn glanced toward the door leading into the hallway that led to the Emergency Room. "Maybe I better have a doctor look at me? Where is the Emergency Room?" he asked and faked a few more coughs. The old woman pointed Thorn in the right direction.

"Where are your parents?" the old woman asked. "I will need to call them."

"I'm eighteen," Thorn lied. "I'll call my parents later. Thanks for your help." Thorn stumbled through the door leading to the ER, let out a few loud coughs, and worked his way into the ER waiting room. He was greeted by a middle-aged woman with short black hair. "I feel sick," Thorn told the woman and plopped down in a wooden chair. If he was being set up—if someone was trying to get him to leave town —then it was his job to remain in town and make sure whoever was trying to get him to leave was going to stay in town as well. "I need to see Dr. Varnell."

Nurse Beth Moist recognized Thorn as one of the preppy students who attended the snotty academy. "Fill out this paperwork," she said, handing Thorn a clipboard full of papers. Thorn took the clipboard and began filling out the forms as Nurse Moist walked back to the examining area and began talking to Dr. Varnell, who was speaking with Rita and Rhonda. "I'm sorry to interrupt, Dr. Varnell, but there is a kid out in the waiting room insisting on seeing you. I think he's one of the students from the Green Valley Academy."

Rita and Rhonda looked at each other. "We were checking to see how Haley was doing before leaving town," Rhonda told Nurse Moist. "Uh...what does this student look like?" Nurse Moist described Thorn. "That's him," Rhonda said in a confused voice.

"Let's go take a look," Rita urged. "Oscar, you stay here."

Dr. Varnell didn't like the expressions on Rita's or Rhonda's faces. He shoved his hands down into a pair of tired trousers and followed Nurse Moist out into the waiting room. Rita and Rhonda stopped at the door leading into the waiting room and peeked out. They spotted Thorn sitting in a wooden chair filling out his paperwork. "He's up to something," Rhonda whispered.

Rita felt a bad feeling enter her gut. "Rhonda, I don't think we're going to be leaving town any time soon."

Rhonda watched Dr. Varnell speak with Thorn. Thorn stood up, handed the clipboard back to Nurse Moist, and then, to everyone's shock, fainted—or so it appeared. Nurse Moist ran back into the examining area and called for extra help. A male nurse darted out into the waiting area and helped Nurse Moist carry Thorn back to an examining room.

As his body passed by Rita and Rhonda, he opened one eye, spotted the two women staring down at him, and then snapped his eye shut.

Rhonda gave a little gasp. "Did you...he..."

"He looked at us," Rita whispered. She grabbed Rhonda's hand and walked out into the waiting area. "Rhonda, tell me again what events took place at the Green Valley Academy."

Rhonda spotted Oscar hurrying out into the waiting area. She rolled her eyes and plopped down in a chair and recounted every second she had spent inside the academy. "I was so certain Thorn Ryeberry took the bait. I read his eyes...I know what I saw..."

Rita sat down next to Rhonda. "I believe you," she promised. "Something must have changed between then and now. But what?"

Oscar sat down next to Rita and began to think. "Maybe the kid is really sick?"

"He's not sick, Oscar," Rita assured Oscar.

"Well," Oscar said, putting his brain to work, "he's here and so are you...maybe that's not a coincidence?"

Rita glanced at Rhonda. "Well?" she asked.

"He opened his eye and looked straight up at us," Rhonda told Rita. "I...think...Oscar may be right this time?" Rhonda put her face in her hands. "We were so close to forcing that skunk to leave town and—" Rhonda stopped. "Leave town... we're here..."

Rita caught on to her sister's thought. "Thorn Ryeberry is trying to keep us in town by having himself admitted to this hospital."

Rhonda raised her head. "Yeah," she said in a frustrated voice. "But how did that weasel outsmart us? He's a seventeen-year-old kid. We're grown women. We have brains...experience and—"

"And that killer has something we don't, Rhonda: a reason for murder. You know as well as I do that a wounded animal will do anything to survive." Rita studied the door leading back to the examining area. "Somehow the killer lurking behind those doors got a step ahead of us. Our duty now is to regroup and figure out what to do." Rita kept her eyes on the door.

"The entire purpose of leading that punk out of town was to protect Mayfield," Rhonda pointed out. "This town truly does need that snotty academy, Sis. You should have seen the inside of that place. It's massive."

Rita bit down on her lip. "Haley Wellington is safe," she said as her mind struggled to form a new plan. "Now all we have to do is lead our killer out of town—but our killer isn't going to leave town. Paula's body is now ashes, which means we lack evidence." Rita looked at Oscar. "We have the missing journal...and that's what we're going to have to work with." Rita closed her eyes and saw the sleepy, snowy town of Mayfield. "If we can catch Thorn Ryeberry in Mayfield..."

"Mayfield will still be connected to the academy," Rhonda pointed out. "And from what Mr. Tulley told me, Mrs. Ryeberry has some major pull. If that woman was angry at one teacher for being hard on her son, can you imagine what she would try to do to a whole town?"

"You're right," Rita said. She rubbed the bridge of her nose. "Which means we still have to try and get Thorn Ryeberry out of town. How to do that is the question."

Dr. Varnell hurried out of the examining room. "He's awake, and he's asking for the woman he talked to at the school," he said. "Alone."

Rhonda stood up. "I'll be back," she told Rita and followed Dr. Varnell into a small, cramped examining room surrounded by depressing green walls.

"Ms. Knight...I must have caught that virus you said Ms. Capperson had," Thorn moaned. "Dr. Varnell...leave us alone...please...I need to tell Ms. Knight...something important..."

"Please give us some privacy," Rhonda told Dr. Varnell. She placed her hand into the pocket of her coat and rested it on her gun. "It's okay."

Dr. Varnell hurried away to call Mayor White. As soon as he closed the door to the examining room, Thorn knocked off his act.

"Every student at Green Valley can testify that you showed up claiming Ms. Capperson was sick. I can ride out all the time I want right here in this hospital, lady."

Rhonda narrowed her eyes. "You killed Paula Capperson, you punk," she snapped.

"Yeah, and you almost had me following you to Georgia," Thorn hissed back. "I spotted you drive away with your twin. I'm not stupid, lady."

"Maybe not, but you are a young, diseased rat that I'm going to send to prison," Rhonda promised. "You'll turn eighteen soon enough, and then you'll spend the rest of your miserable life behind bars."

Thorn felt his cheeks turn red. "I'm going to spend the rest of my life married to a rich woman, lady," he growled. "I'm going to spend the rest of my life partying on yachts and living it up." Thorn pointed a dangerous finger at Rhonda. "This stupid town has caused me a lot of headaches, lady. I'm about to end my headaches, beginning with Haley Wellington. I know people. I can have Haley killed. Unless you give me the missing journal and take a hike, she's dead. Got it?"

Rhonda slapped Thorn's finger out of the air with a hard hand. "Listen to me, you little twerp," she growled back, "you don't scare me, do you hear me? So go call your momma and whine to her because by the time I'm through with you, all you're going to be able to do is whine...behind bars...for life."

"You're dead," Thorn promised Rhonda.

Rhonda put her nose to Thorn's face. "No, dear," she

promised, "you're the one who's dead." She then walked out of the examining room, leaving Thorn fuming. "Not smart," Rhonda whispered, "you lost your temper with a little snot... not smart." Rhonda spotted Dr. Varnell on the phone. She bowed her head and closed her eyes. "Rita and I can just walk away...but we can't. So the only question is...now what?"

As Rhonda stood in the examining area, Billy walked into the Emergency Room soaked with snow.

Billy shook snow off his heavy brown coat. "Boy, snow is falling worse than Georgia rain on a stormy day," he mumbled to himself as he began kicking snow off his boots.

"Billy?" Rita said, her mouth open. She rushed over to him. "You're early!"

Billy took off his ball cap, shook snow off, and slapped the cap back down on his head. "I took a plane," he explained. "I left Chester at one of them dog hotels, too. Boy, that dog sure gave me a mean eye." Billy shook his head. "On the way home I have to stop, get my truck out of the airport parking, and grab Chester. Can't say I'm looking forward to it. Chester is going to be one grumpy dog."

Rita softly hugged Billy. "Thank you for arriving so quickly, Billy. I'm very happy to see you."

"Oh, wasn't nothing," Billy promised and hugged Rita back. Then his eyes went to a short, funny-looking man who was staring at him. "Who are you, fella?"

Oscar straightened his back. "Oscar Frost is my name, Jack. You're hugging my woman," he said in a gruff voice.

"Jack? Why, my name is Billy Northfield," Billy told Oscar. He looked at Rita. "Do you know this fella?"

Rita sighed. "I'm afraid I do," she explained. "Billy, this is Oscar. Oscar, this is Billy...my...boyfriend."

Oscar's jaw dropped. "Boyfriend?"

Rita nudged Billy with her elbow. "Yes, my boyfriend," she said in a loving, sincere voice.

"Well, I'll be." Billy smiled.

Oscar frowned. "A boyfriend isn't a husband...so there's still hope, hot stuff," he told Rita. "I shall win your love." Oscar narrowed his eyes at Billy. "From this moment forward, you and I are at war." Oscar walked up to Billy, threw back his right boot, and kicked Billy in his left leg as hard as he could. Rita winced.

"Hey..." Billy yelped. He grabbed his leg and began rubbing it. "What's the matter with you...you got flies in your brain?"

"Uh...Oscar...I wouldn't," Rita warned.

Oscar ignored Rita. "I shall defend the woman I love," he announced and began to kick Billy again.

Billy threw out his right hand and grabbed Oscar by his throat. "Scram before I slap you senseless, boy."

Oscar's face turned red. His eyes grew wide. "Okay," he whimpered. Billy let go of his throat. "The...war isn't over," Oscar promised as he quickly backed away from Billy. "I shall win my woman's love."

Billy looked at Oscar as though the little man had termites eating at his brain. "You on some kind of medicine?" he asked. Rita grinned. "Maybe I should go find you a doctor."

Oscar glared at Billy—at a safe distance, of course. "Listen, hillbilly. My intelligence can run rings around your backwoods brain. So why don't you drive back down south and play your banjo and count how many teeth you've got left in your mouth."

Billy touched his jaw. "Why, I've got all of my teeth, fella. I see Dr. Dalton every three months." Rita fought back a sweet giggle. "And I don't play no banjo. Why, my daddy taught me to play the guitar. Reckon I ain't the greatest but I can sure play 'Amazing Grace' as pretty as you like."

Oscar stared at Billy. He had to admit Billy didn't seem

like too bad of a guy. But all was fair in love and war. "Oh, go back home, hillbilly. Go wind up your rooster or something."

"Wind up my rooster?" Billy asked, confused. "Why, that old rooster would tear me a new backside if I messed with him. Meanest rooster I've ever had. I ain't gonna go messing with him." Billy looked at Rita. "This little fella has flies in his brain."

Rita let a giggle slip. Billy and Oscar had finally officially met. "Billy—"

"Don't defend me, my love," Oscar cried out. "I am Jack, and I shall slay the giant living at the top of the beanstalk!" Oscar pointed at Billy. "High noon tomorrow...we duel, giant!"

Billy slowly folded his arms together. "Funny little guy, ain't he?" he asked Rita. "Maybe he escaped from one of them mental homes?"

Oscar frowned and began to throw an insult back at Billy —then he simply felt the air leave his balloon and plopped down in a chair. "I'm doing it again," he told Rita. "I'm making a complete stranger think I'm crazy."

"Well...yes," Rita told Oscar. She walked over to him and patted his shoulder. "Oscar, all you have to do is be yourself. Billy is a terrific guy. You would really like him if you opened up and tried."

Oscar lifted his eyes, studied Rita's beautiful face, and then looked over at Billy. "Sorry I kicked you."

"Oh, nothing to be sorry about," Billy told Oscar. "My momma once told me a man does all kinds of crazy stuff when he's smitten with a woman." Billy walked over to Oscar and held out his hand. "Billy Northfield is my name and farming is my game."

Oscar looked up into Billy's kind eyes and saw a decent man. "Oscar Frost is my name. Being a jerk...was my game," he said and shook Billy's hand. As he did, a strong feeling of friendship resonated from Billy and entered his heart. "I guess you can tell I like to write books."

Billy nodded. "Libraries would be a mighty boring place if folks didn't like to write books," he told Oscar. "And—" Rhonda walked out into the waiting room before he could continue.

"Billy!" Rhonda called out in a surprised voice. She ran over and hugged him with loving arms. "Oh, it's so great to see you and—" Rhonda stopped short as Zach walked into the waiting room and began kicking snow off his boots. "Zach?"

"Figured you could use all the help you could get," Billy explained and patted Rhonda's hand. "Had Zach fly up. I was mighty happy when his plane was only a few hours behind mine. Didn't have to wait long at all. No sir."

Zach looked at Rhonda with tired eyes. "Hey," he said in an uncertain voice. "Uh, Billy asked me to come. I hope that's okay."

Rita studied her sister's eyes. Rhonda was very happy to see Zach. "Good for you, Sis," she whispered.

Rhonda walked over to Zach and smiled at him. The poor guy was wearing a gray coat that was much too thin. "We're going to have to get you a new coat."

"Yeah...I kinda rushed to the airport," Zach explained. He removed his ball cap and looked at Rhonda. He was sure happy to see her. "Billy told me there's trouble?"

"Murder," Rhonda told Zach and then, without understanding how it happened, she reached out and hugged Zach. To her relief, Zach returned the embrace. "It's good to see you again."

Zach let go of Rhonda. He looked deeply into her beautiful eyes. "What's happening?" he asked.

"Trouble, turkey," Oscar said and then caught his tongue. "Uh...murder," he said and looked up at Rita. "Sorry."

Rita patted Oscar's shoulder. "Better." She smiled.

Rhonda looked at Oscar. "Much better," she agreed.

Billy glanced around the waiting room. "Reckon there might be a snack bar in this place?" he asked. "Them peanuts I ate on the plane didn't do any good."

"We can go to the café and eat," Oscar suggested. "I'm kinda hungry myself."

"I'm starved," Rhonda confessed. She looked at Rita with worried eyes. "We might as well eat because our killer isn't going anywhere." Rhonda walked over to a chair and sat down. "Thorn Ryeberry threatened to kill Haley Wellington unless we give him the missing journal he's been searching for."

"Why don't you call Sheriff O'Neil?" Oscar asked.

"Because Thorn Ryeberry has a mother who can buy an army of lawyers," Rhonda explained. "It's my word against his. Besides, we have your little town to protect, Oscar."

"Oh, you called me Oscar," Oscar sighed. "You didn't call me squirt or runt or twerp. Progress is being made."

"Don't count on it. I still have to scald my lips with bleach," Rhonda told Oscar.

"Ah, but what a kiss," Oscar sighed again.

"Kiss?" Zach asked, not looking happy.

"It was nothing, I'll explain later," Rhonda moaned. "Right now, we're between a rock and a hard place."

"You see," Rita began to speak, "Rhonda and I are trying to do everything within our power to—" Rita stopped as Mayor White hurried through the front entrance doors. He spotted Rita and Rhonda and hurried over to them. "Mayor White?"

"Please, get out of town," Mayor White begged Rita. "Take your friends and leave."

Rita looked into a pair of angry and frantic eyes. "I'm sorry, that's not possible."

"You're going to destroy this town!" Mayor White told Rita in a desperate voice.

"My sister and I are doing everything within our power to *save* your town while catching a killer," Rita told him. "Mayor White, my sister and I could simply slap a pair of cuffs on Thorn Ryeberry this very second. My sister saw him running from Paula Capperson's home. She heard him threaten to kill Haley Wellington. Mr. Tulley, the headmaster at Green Valley Academy, even admitted that the punk was troublesome and that his mother was trying to get Paula Capperson fired."

"I don't think Thorn's mother can have the academy shut down all on her own," Rhonda told Mayor White. "However, Paula Capperson did steal a lot of personal information on different parents and students. My concern is that those other parents will be the ones who pull their children from the academy. Mr. Tulley told me he was preparing to reveal the truth to the parents."

"What?" Mayor White gasped. "But we spoke...he said he wouldn't...I paid him..." Mayor White froze.

"You paid him?" Rita asked.

Mayor White's face crumpled up into a painful knot. He blew out a great sigh. "Okay...okay..." he confessed and looked down at the gray overcoat covering his shaking body. "Mr. Tulley blackmailed the town. He knew Paula Capperson was stealing private information, and he allowed her to do so."

"But Mr. Tulley told me he caught Paula stealing private information," Rhonda said. "He seemed very sincere."

"Of course he caught Paula Capperson stealing the information," Mayor White told Rhonda. "But he didn't stop her. Oh, he played the good guy through it all, but trust me... that awful man is an ugly snake." Billy and Zach looked at each other. Billy shrugged his shoulders and focused back on Mayor White. "Mr. Tulley knew if Paula Capperson's criminal deeds reached the ears of certain parents...all of the parents, to be honest...they would yank their children from the academy and close it down. So what does the rat do? He threatens me…forces me to pay him blackmail money…and lets Paula Capperson continue on her little adventure."

Rita rubbed her chin. "Paula was stealing private information in order to protect her job," she pointed out. "I don't think she was trying to openly violate any rules. Yet, down the line she must have come across some very personal information." Rita looked at Oscar. "Oscar, we have to read the journal you have."

"No," Mayor White begged. "Please, just leave my town and leave well enough alone."

"We're not going to let Thorn Ryeberry get away with murder, Mayor White," Rita snapped. She was losing her patience. "An innocent woman is dead. Her killer is right behind those doors. Haley Wellington nearly killed herself. And through it all my sister and I are jumping through hoops to make sure some silly, snooty school stays open in order to help your town." Rita placed her hands on her hips. Rhonda winced. Whenever Rita put her hands on her hips it meant a storm was coming. "Listen, you little whine bag. Haley Wellington will talk…sooner or later. Right now, the poor girl is far too weak. When she does talk, her testimony will be enough to destroy Thorn Ryeberry. That boy knows that and he's threatened to kill Haley Wellington! So when does it stop? Huh?" she snapped. "How many have to die before you stop trying to protect a killer?" Rita stared at Mayor White with fuming eyes. "How many, Mayor White?"

"I…have my town to protect," Mayor White whimpered. He nodded at Rhonda. "Your sister is right…Mrs. Ryeberry can't close the academy down alone. Thorn Ryeberry called my cell phone about twenty minutes ago. He threatened to turn over all of Paula Capperson's journals if I don't make you leave town. If that woman's journals reach the hands of angry parents, they'll close the academy. If Thorn Ryeberry is arrested for murder, he'll turn over the journals for certain." Mayor White ran his hands through his gray hair. "The political atmosphere is so delicate," he tried to explain. "If one student fumbles the ball, the rest are taken out of the game. Even if Thorn Ryeberry didn't have Paula Capperson's private journals...simply arresting him for murder would cause an avalanche of panic. Can't you realize that?"

"So what are we supposed to do? Let a killer walk free?" Rita asked in a shocked voice.

"Mrs. Ryeberry is leaving London as we speak," Mayor White whimpered. "She's coming to take her son out of the country. Thorn Ryeberry will never be seen again. Our... troubles will be over. Now please...leave my town."

"Does Thorn Ryeberry know his mother is on her way to Vermont?" Rita asked.

Mayor White shook his head. "No. But she is a very angry lady who will do anything needed to protect her son. She is worried that if her son finds out she has left London he will act foolishly." Mayor White drew in a scared breath. "Mrs. Ryeberry is not pleased with her son. If...she can simply take him away, the academy will be saved. Please."

Rita looked at Rhonda. "Looks like we're in a pinch," she said.

"Looks like every single game plan we created has been tossed out the window." Rhonda blew out a breath. "I guess it's time to stop trying to be nice and start being cops."

"What are you talking about?" Mayor White asked.

"What my sister means is we tried to help you protect your town, Mayor White. We bent every rule in the book to do so. But now it's time to stop playing nice." Rita pulled out her gun. "Mayor White, get Sheriff O'Neil over here and I mean now. Rhonda, come on, we're going to arrest our killer."

Mayor White panicked. "No..." he whimpered. He yanked out a cell phone and called Sheriff O'Neil. "Sheriff, you have to stop them...hurry."

Rita and Rhonda charged back into the examining area

with Billy, Zach, and Oscar following them. They marched into Thorn's room with their guns at the ready. "Hands in the air!" Rhonda yelled at Thorn. Thorn looked into Rhonda's eyes. The eyes he looked into clearly said: "One wrong move and you're dead." He quickly raised his hands into the air.

"You're making a fatal mistake, lady!" Thorn yelled at Rhonda. "Do you hear me!"

"My only mistake was trying to bend the rules in order to play Ms. Nice," Rhonda told Thorn as she fished a pair of handcuffs out of her coat pocket. "Rita, do the honors."

Far away, zooming through the air, Mrs. Angela Ryeberry called her husband. "I'm going to get Thorn."

"Kill him," a hard voice said. "He's become a liability."

"What? I will n—"

"Kill the boy or die yourself. I know all about your secret meetings, Angela. You have one choice to live. Make it count," the voice snapped and ended the call. Angela Ryeberry put down her phone with a shaky hand.

"I'm...sorry," she whispered. "Thorn, you...have to die."

chapter seven

Sheriff O'Neil walked Thorn down a short wooden hallway and placed him in a holding cell. "He's still a minor," he explained. "I've called the academy. Mr. Tulley is contacting his parents," he told Rita and Rhonda in a worried voice.

"His mother is already flying in from London," Rhonda told Sheriff O'Neil.

Thorn glared at Rhonda. "I'll be out and free," he warned her. "I don't forget."

Rhonda watched Thorn plop down on a cot, toss his arms behind his head, and close his eyes. "Come on," she told Rita.

Rita followed Rhonda back into a medium-sized room with a hardwood floor and wooden walls. The room smelled of hot coffee, donuts, and dust. Billy, Zach, and Oscar were standing near a closed door that opened up into the cramped office Sheriff O'Neil was forced to call home. "Where did Mayor White go?" she asked.

"Back to his office, or so he claimed," Zach told Rita. He lifted up a brown coffee cup. "Coffee?"

"No, thanks," Rita said. "Sis, coffee?"

Rhonda shook her head. "I don't like Mayor White roaming around free," she remarked in an uneasy voice. She shoved her hands down into the pockets of her coat and looked around the room. She counted three desks sitting in a semicircle. Each desk held a phone, a computer, and a desk calendar. The desks looked as if they had never been sat at. "Don't forget it was Mayor White who had Paula's body cremated. There's no telling what he might try and do now."

"What can he do?" Sheriff O'Neil asked. "Ms. Knight, we have the killer in custody. Mr. Tulley has assured me that he is going to keep this incident very silent for tonight as to not cause any alarm among the students. All that is left to do is wait for Mrs. Ryeberry to show up while I write up the charges." Sheriff O'Neil looked down at his cold hands. His coat began to drip snow onto the hardwood floor. "I didn't want to help Barney," he said, calling Mayor White by his first name. "I assumed the situation would spiral out of control. When Haley Wellington ended up at the hospital I...I should have arrested the kid. I was wrong not to." Sheriff O'Neil kept his eyes low. "I know the academy provides a lot of work for Mayfield. I know families need food on their table. I also know justice must not be perverted. I...the greater cause outweighed my ability to perform my duty..."

"We were all trying to prevent a small town from caving under," Rita assured Sheriff O'Neil. "Rhonda and I did everything within our power to draw Thorn Ryeberry out of Mayfield in order to arrest him. We were going to force him to try and kill one of us in order to nab him on a different murder charge. Our plan failed."

"Wouldn't have mattered," Sheriff O'Neil told Rita in a tired voice. "I looked into that boy's eyes. He's evil." Sheriff O'Neil looked toward his office. "I need to go write up the charges. I have Gary and Mitchell up at the academy guarding the entrance. Mr. Tulley requested I do so." Sheriff O'Neil offered a weak smile and went into his office.

Billy turned worried eyes on Rita. "You girls were going to do an awful dangerous thing," he said.

"Yeah," Zach agreed. "Playing bait isn't a good idea."

"We were trying to help this town," Rhonda explained. "We failed. That killer sitting back there stole all of Paula's journals. All he has to do is make them public and Green Valley Academy will die." Rhonda sighed. "The odds were against us. But...at least we have our killer."

"For how long?" Rita asked, her brow furrowed. "Sis, you know as well as I do all we have is your word against his."

"And the journal," Oscar added. He reached under his coat and pulled out a red journal. "I went back to my apartment after I left the hospital and got the journal. There's...more in here than I told you. I...was kinda being a jerk. But now I know how important it is. Here." Oscar handed the journal to Rita.

Rita looked at Oscar with proud eyes. "You're a real gentleman," she said and kissed his cheek.

"Wow...real love," Oscar gasped as his cheeks turned red. "Marry me...oh, marry me, please."

"Oh, brother." Rhonda rolled her eyes. "Cool it, Romeo. It's only the first date."

"Excitable little fella, ain't he?" Billy said to Zach. Zach nodded.

"Oscar, honey, why don't you go home. I'll call you if I need you." Rita smiled. She patted Oscar's shoulder.

"I think I'll go to the café and have a slice of pie first." Oscar smiled back. "Maple is still on duty."

"Oscar," Rita warned.

"I'll be a gentleman," Oscar promised. "Well...maybe," he quickly added and hurried over to the wooden front door. "That journal is your key to success," he explained, becoming very serious. "There's a riddle in there that I can't figure out. If you can figure out the riddle, I think you'll find the treasure you need."

"Riddle?" Rita said. "Seriously?"

Oscar nodded, slapped on his gloves, and opened the

front door. "I'll call you tomorrow. I know I'm in the way right now and of no real help." And with those words, he slipped out into the snowy day.

"Riddle?" Rita said again. She motioned Rhonda over to her. "Uh, guys, why don't you go find the café and get us some food?" she asked. "Rhonda and I have some reading to do."

Billy looked at Zach. "I can eat."

"Me, too." Zach nodded.

"Then let's go." Billy tipped his hat at Rita and Rhonda and walked out into the snow with Zach. He bumped right into Oscar. "I thought you were leaving."

"Are you nuts?" Oscar whispered. He grabbed Billy's hand and tugged him away from the front door, waited for a red truck to ease down the snowy street, and looked across the street at a small courthouse. "Listen, Jack—"

"My name is Billy, and I don't live up on no beanstalk," Billy told Oscar.

"Yeah…uh, sorry," Oscar said, catching his tongue as an icy wind slapped at the brown winter hat he was wearing. "Old habits…bad nature."

Zach stepped close to Oscar. He tucked his head low, wishing he had on a warmer coat. "What's on your mind?" he asked.

"Murder," Oscar said in an obvious voice. "Look, guys, I've read every one of Paula Capperson's journals. I know what's going on up at Green Valley Academy. I know what type of kids attend the school and who the parents are. We're talking some real serious sharp knives, here."

Billy looked down at Oscar. "Throw some dirt on the mud for us."

Oscar glanced around. "Thorn Ryeberry is supposed to marry the daughter of a very high-ranking European Union official," he whispered. "This guy has some major power over the European banks. We're talking about billions upon billions of dollars and a pocket full of power." Oscar glanced around. "But this guy is small change compared to the real suits," he said. "Thorn Ryeberry and his folks...mere pennies in the bank. But..." Oscar glanced around again. "If you play the game right...well, you can move up the ladder."

"Play the game?" Billy asked, ignoring the freezing snow and wind.

"Sure, sure," Oscar explained. "In America we have two political parties, right? Sure, we do. It's no different in Europe. Folks over there get after each other's throats the same way Americans do when it comes times to vote. But the secret is, both parties are the same. It's all a scam."

"I'm not following," Zach told Oscar.

"Look," Oscar said, "Thorn Ryeberry was attached to the daughter of a very powerful crook in order to start forming a new party while the people of Europe still think they're trapped in the old warehouse."

"You getting this?" Billy asked Zach. He rubbed the back of his neck. "I ain't following you, little fella."

Oscar shook his head and resisted calling Billy a hillbilly. "Look...it's like the changing of the guards," he explained. "Europe is slowly being transformed into a socialist state. Why in the world do you think every country in Europe is being flooded with migrants? Folks are trying to destroy the European identity and form a completely new union of countries controlled by one central body. But in order to do so there has to be a changing of the guards. Out with the old and in with the new. Mr. Ryeberry is the new. The guy is a complete communist who is faithful to anarchy. Somehow he's rubbed hands with some very powerful people who have agreed to accept him into their little club and even allow him to marry off his son to the daughter of a very important man."

"How do you know all of this?" Zach asked. "Did Ms. Capperson write all of this down in her journals?"

"Nope," Oscar said in a proud voice. "Paula, dear sweet but hideous Paula, hacked into private emails that dear old mommy was sending her precious little boy. Dear old mommy was telling her little boy some very delicate information. Why? Because dear old mommy and her son seemed to be working on the opposing team."

"Mrs. Ryeberry was going against her husband?" Zach asked.

Oscar nodded. "Paula knew this. She stored the information away." Oscar glanced around. "She didn't write any of this in her journals, though. She let me read the emails, sure. She printed them out, but I don't have a clue as to where she hid them. The journals she kept are damaging...and may do the trick. But if not, guys, we have to find those emails."

Zach looked at Billy and then back at Oscar. "What was the riddle you mentioned to Rita and Rhonda?"

"A bunch of numbers that I can't make sense of," Oscar explained. "I guess it doesn't matter? I mean, look, if word got out that Thorn Ryeberry was dating a local girl and reached the ears of the man who was marrying off his daughter to him...that would be all she wrote. The wedding would be called off and dear old daddy would be kicked out of the club." Oscar glanced around again to make sure no one was listening. "Dear old mommy wants to make sure her little boy marries the daughter of her enemy in order to infiltrate the enemy's camp. That's why Thorn Ryeberry is going through so much trouble to find the missing journal. That's why he killed Paula. And that's why he will probably try and kill Haley Wellington."

"Did you tell Rita or Rhonda any of this?" Zach asked.

"No way," Oscar told Zach. "Look, guys, if you get tangled up with hard people then you get hit even harder. The journal I gave my two sweet loves only contains information about Thorn dating Haley Wellington and other little interesting tidbits that can destroy Thorn Ryeberry's future and cause some serious problems. But," Oscar lowered his voice, "there's nothing incriminating enough to cause a war. Sure, Thorn Ryeberry and his folks would be tossed into the gutter, but so what? But man, if those emails ever were made public...wow. That's why I didn't tell my two loves. It's bad enough they're tangling with Thorn Ryeberry as it is. But what can I do about it? At first, I thought it was fun and decided to write a good story off this mess...but the more I got to know my two loves...oh, I can't let them dig the holes they're standing in any deeper than they are."

Zach rubbed his nose. "Okay...let me try to make sense of all this. A teacher, fearing for her job, gathered illegal data on students and parents in order to secure her job? Right?"

"Right so far."

"Then one of the students, this Ryeberry kid, who starts holding hands with a local girl he wasn't supposed to be seeing for political reasons, kills his teacher. Right?" Zach asked. Oscar nodded. "Mayor White is afraid Green Valley Academy will be shut down if the kid is charged with murder?"

"Yep," Oscar confirmed.

"So Rita and Rhonda try to trick the kid into leaving town...use themselves as bait...in order to get the kid to try to kill them?" Oscar nodded yes. "They were going to try and secure this trap because Mayor White and some of his friends, in haste, had Paula Capperson's body cremated."

"No body, no evidence," Oscar pointed out. "My two loves are not about to let a killer run free. That's why they were willing to become bait. Also, because my two loves have such tender hearts, they were honestly trying to protect this little town from losing a big chunk of gold."

Zach shook his head and looked at Billy. "A girl tried to kill herself. I'm sure these people aren't going to leave her alone."

"Not from the sound of it." Billy nodded. "Sounds to me

like we have a bunch of wild dogs running loose that will hunt down any wounded animal standing in their way."

"Look," Oscar said in a serious voice, "I'm going to keep a close eye on my two loves. When Mrs. Ryeberry shows up, there's going to be some major fireworks going off. If anyone tries to hurt my sweet babies I'll come to their rescue, okay? I have this. I really do."

"No offense," Zach told Oscar, "you're not an intimating sort of guy."

"No, but I have this." Oscar pulled a can of bear spray out from the front pocket of his coat.

Billy examined the bear spray. "Ah, that's just mouthwash," he fussed. Oscar frowned. "Now, don't go getting all upset on me," Billy told Oscar. "Besides, three bears on watch instead of one is much better. The only thing I'm wondering about is what in the world we need to be doing here?"

Zach stared at the front door leading into the sheriff's station. "I guess we need to tell Rita and Rhonda the truth."

"Are you crazy?" Oscar complained. "Look, the less our two beauties know, the better they'll be off. I may not be a knight in shining armor, but I'm not stupid enough to get two beautiful women killed. And my guess is," Oscar lowered his voice, "that kid inside that jail...his days are numbered."

Billy and Zach looked down at Oscar. Oscar simply nodded and then put his bear spray away.

Rita closed the journal she and Rhonda were reading, tossed it down on the desk she was sitting at, and rubbed her eyes. "If I understand correctly," she told Rhonda, "Paula recorded enough information to embarrass the Ryeberry family."

"Haley Wellington was blackmailing Thorn Ryeberry." Rhonda whistled. "My, my, for a small town there sure is a lot of drama taking place. And I thought Clovedale Falls had drama...sheesh." Rhonda walked over to a cozy coffee station and studied a brown coffee cup sitting on a gray saucer. "Coffee?"

"No, thank you." Rita stopped rubbing her eyes. "Haley Wellington was forcing Thorn Ryeberry to pay her money."

"Oscar did say the girl wasn't innocent," Rhonda pointed out. She picked up the coffee cup. "I wonder if Mrs. Ryeberry knew."

Rita watched her sister prepare a cup of coffee. "I doubt it."

"Yeah," Rhonda agreed. "If Mrs. Ryeberry did know, I'm sure our killer wouldn't be sitting behind bars right now." Rhonda decided to add some cream and sugar to her coffee instead of drinking it black. "I guess Haley Wellington freaked out when she heard Paula had been killed. Maybe she feared Thorn Ryeberry was going to come for her? Maybe her daddy gave her a few choice words? Maybe her emotions caved in? Who knows? But what I do know—and fear—is that Haley Wellington isn't out of danger yet."

Rita agreed. "So what do we do?" she wondered.

"Hide that journal," Rhonda pointed out.

Rita looked around the front room. "Well," she said, "let's be smart and plant the cow right in front of everyone's nose."

Rhonda watched Rita begin ripping out each page of the journal. When that chore was complete, Rita opened the top righthand desk drawer, pulled out a stack of printing paper, placed the paper into the journal, and then tucked the journal pages under the printing paper. "Smart."

Rita picked up the red journal, looked around again, and hurried over to a wooden filing cabinet. A single plastic evidence bag was sitting on top of the filing cabinet that one of Sheriff O'Neil's deputies had been using to store donuts in. Rita tossed the journal into the bag and then placed the bag back down on the desk she had been sitting at. Next she found a black marker and wrote the word "EVIDENCE" across the front on large, bold letters. "We'll leave this bag sitting exactly where it is."

Rhonda nodded. "In the meantime, we need to call Mr. Wellington and tell him not to leave his daughter's side."

"Wouldn't hurt," Rita agreed and began reaching for a phone. As she did, Mayor White burst through the front doors wearing a panic-stricken face.

"I told you!" Mayor White yelled at Rita and Rhonda. "I told you...oh my...I told you!"

Sheriff O'Neil came rushing out of his office. "Barney... what's the matter? What's wrong?"

"Mr. Tulley called me," Mayor White nearly screamed. "He has called every single parent and informed them of the truth. My phone has been ringing off the hook. Parents are calling me from all over the globe demanding answers." Mayor White looked at Rita and Rhonda with sour eyes. "You two have destroyed my town!"

Billy stepped in through the front door. "Watch your mouth, mister," he warned Mayor White.

Mayor White looked at Billy, saw Zach step in behind him, and then saw Oscar. "You," he pointed at Oscar in a furious voice, "you and that woman...this is all your fault!" The cell phone in Mayor White's pocket rang. "Not again," he cried and quickly answered the call. "Yes...Mr. Gables...yes...no, I assure you Ms. Capperson was not murdered. Yes, I know what Mr. Tulley told you...no...your son is perfectly safe. Well, yes...Thorn Ryeberry has been taken into custody....no...please, there is no need to leave New Zealand, Mr. Gables...hello...hello?" Mayor White threw his eyes at Rita and Rhonda. "See...see!" he yelled.

"Oh, put a sock in it," Rhonda snapped. "You better be happy my sister and I haven't reported you and your friends to the state for illegally cremating the body of Paula Capperson."

"That's right," Rita said in a firm voice. "My sister and I turned a blind eye in order to assist this town. The pieces are falling apart, though, and now it's time to end this mess." Rita pointed toward the holding area. "That kid isn't walking away free, do you hear me? He's going to pay the price for killing Paula Capperson."

"Ms. Knight is right, Barney," Sheriff O' Neil told his friend. "We should have been straightforward from the beginning."

Mayor White spotted the evidence bag holding Paula Capperson's journal. "Is that one of those awful journals?"

"Why, yes." Rita nodded. She picked up the journal and handed it to Sheriff O'Neil. "Please secure this journal."

"I'll put it in my office," Sheriff O'Neil assured Rita and hurried away.

"Mayor White," Rita said, "as complicated as this situation may seem, it's not very hard to understand. Now, what matters the most is bringing a solid conviction against Thorn Ryeberry. And if my sister and I had not been so gullible, we would have carried out duties in the proper manner from the start. Now, go back to your office and manage the worries of concerned parents like a responsible mayor."

"You don't understand," Mayor White snapped at Rita. "Mrs. Ryeberry will be here soon. She's not going to be happy. She's going to walk right out of this jail with her son. You destroyed my town for nothing...nothing. Oh..." Mayor White stormed out of the front door.

"He's right, you know," Rhonda said in a concerned voice. "Thorn Ryeberry is still considered a minor. We don't have any concrete evidence to hold him on except for the contents of the journal, but any lawyer can have the contents dismissed in a court of law, claiming privacy laws were violated."

"And I doubt Haley Wellington is going to jump at the

chance to testify," Rita added. She rubbed her eyes again. "Rhonda, we can't let that killer walk out of here."

Rhonda wasn't sure what to do. She knew that Angela Ryeberry was going to walk out of the jail with her son...a killer...a deadly person...a minor...a kid...an inexperienced kid. "Rita, Thorn Ryeberry isn't smarter than us," she said. "I need a tape recorder. Hurry."

Rita stared at Rhonda and then simply let out a heavy breath. "Boy, are we dumb. We were overthinking things again."

Rhonda shrugged her shoulders. "This is only our second day in town...we deserve a break."

Oscar eased forward, reached into his front pocket, and pulled out a small tape recorder. "I...was recording your voices...to remember you by." He blushed. "You two dolls have the prettiest voices I've ever heard...please don't be mad."

Rita took the tape recorder from Oscar with grateful hands. "We're not mad," she assured the embarrassed little man.

Zach looked at Rhonda. "You're going to go talk to the kid?" he asked.

"Yep," Rhonda said and took the tape recorder from her sister and checked it. "I'm going to get myself a confession and—" Rhonda read something in Zach's eyes that worried her. "What is it?" she asked.

"Don't," Oscar warned Zach.

"Don't what?" Rhonda demanded.

Rita looked at Billy. "Billy?"

Billy kicked at the wooden floor with his boot. "Well, it's like this," he said and looked at Zach for help. "You know how to speak all them fancy words. You explain what that little fella told us outside."

"No," Oscar demanded. "I told you—"

"Oscar, when you care for someone, you tell them the

truth," Zach explained. "I know you mean well, and I appreciate it, but Rita and Rhonda need to know the truth."

Oscar sighed. "Sure...go ahead and put a bull's-eye on their back."

"What is Oscar talking about?" Rhonda asked.

Zach walked over to one of the desks, sat down on the edge, folded his arms, and began to carefully relay, in his own words, everything Oscar had confessed to him while standing outside in the snow. "I guess those emails might be a good way to stop this Angela Ryeberry woman in her tracks?"

Oscar shook his head. "And create a deadly enemy."

"Can't run from a snake, little fella," Billy told Oscar. "A snake sure can bite hard, but a person has to be able to kill it." Billy looked at Rita. "Sure would help if you girls could find them missing emails."

"Sure would," Rhonda agreed in an urgent voice.

Rita grabbed Rhonda's coffee and took a drink. "Too much sugar," she complained. Rhonda shrugged. "Where would Paula have hidden those emails?"

Rhonda looked at Oscar. "Oscar, do you have any idea?"

"Not a clue," Oscar answered honestly.

Billy walked over to the coffee station and studied the set-up. He decided to make himself a cup of coffee. As he did, his mind began thinking about a riddle. "Say," he said, "did you girls ever figure out that there riddle?" Billy turned around. "You know, the riddle the little fella told you was in the journal?"

"No, sorry," Rita told Billy in a disappointed voice. "Rhonda and I came across a set of numbers, but we couldn't make sense of them."

"The numbers were written under a journal entry containing information about Haley Wellington blackmailing Thorn Ryeberry. I thought the numbers might have been numbers attached to a bank account, but it didn't match."

"Not enough numbers to be a banking number and too

many numbers to be a phone number or a combination to a lock," Rita added.

"Maybe a password?" Zach suggested.

Rhonda threw her eyes at Zach. "A password?" she asked.

"Could be?" Zach suggested. "I use only numbers when I create a password. At the end of my password, I add a character...sometimes a period or an exclamation mark. I had a computer friend tell me—"

"The numbers," Rhonda told Rita.

"There were two exclamation marks after the last number," Rita announced. She drained Rhonda's coffee. "Rhonda, you stay here with Zach and work on getting a confession out of Thorn Ryeberry. Billy and I will hurry to Paula's home and try to see if we can access her computer. It could be Paula has all the emails saved on her computer?"

"What about the hard copies?" Zach asked.

"I'm not sure," Rita confessed. "One step at a time."

"Well, I guess we better get a move on," Billy told Rita. "Little fella, you better stay here and guard this door with that there bear spray you have. No one comes in or leaves until I get back."

Oscar felt a sudden sense of pride wash over him. Someone was actually depending on him...trusting him. Sure, he knew Rita and Rhonda were digging the hole they were standing in even deeper—at least in his opinion—but what could he do about it? The only option was to stand brave and protect his two loves. "You got it, Billy," he said, yanking out his can of bear spray. "I'll guard the door, my dear friend. I'll post my courage into the open skies and let it rain down like the morning dew. I'll stand like an iron sword prepared to battle any foe that dares to challenge my battle-ready heart. Oh yes, my friend, Oscar Frost will defend his newfound family against the darkest depths and the highest dangers. I—"

"We get it, we get it." Rhonda rolled her eyes. "Oscar, we get it."

Sheriff O'Neil quickly exited his office. He frowned at everyone. "I have to get up to the academy."

"Why?" Rita asked.

"Mr. Tulley called me. Parents are demanding I station myself at the academy and wait for their arrival." Sheriff O'Neil checked his squeaky voice. "I'm only an insurance salesman. I'm not meant for all of this excitement."

"You better go," Rita said in a sorrowful voice, feeling sorry for Sheriff O'Neil.

"I'm leaving you two in charge," Sheriff O'Neil told Rita and Rhonda. "I've already run you both through the system. You two are accomplished cops. Hope you don't mind that I ran you? I had to be safe."

"We're not offended," Rita assured Sheriff O'Neil.

Sheriff O'Neil looked at Billy, Zach, and Oscar. "You two men are now deputized, too. And you," he told Oscar and winced, "well, you seem to be educated in this mess...you can man the phones."

"Gee, thanks." Oscar frowned.

"Okay...okay," Sheriff O'Neil said and rubbed his temples, "what have I got to lose?" He locked eyes with Oscar. "Oscar, you're...now deputized, too. Your job is to man the phones and make sure no one, and I mean no one except the people standing in this room goes back to see the prisoner until I get back."

"Can I wear a gun...huh, huh?" Oscar asked and nearly began bouncing around. "First Billy trusts me and now you... wow, this is a really good day for me."

"Uh...no gun." Sheriff O'Neil winced. He pointed at the bear spray Oscar was holding. "That weapon is good enough." And with those words, Sheriff O'Neil hurried away on wobbly legs.

"Poor man," Rhonda said, watching the sheriff step out into the snow.

"I know," Rita sighed. She looked at Billy. "Ready?"

Billy heard his stomach growl. He sure was hungry. "Wouldn't mind if we stopped on the way and grabbed a burger. Maybe this here town has one of them Chick-Fil-A's we like?"

"Oh, Billy," Rita said, grabbing Billy's hand and dragging him over to the front door. "Rhonda, two hours, tops. If we're not back by then, that means we've encountered trouble."

"Two hours. Got it, Sis."

Rita nodded and pulled Billy out into the snow.

"I wouldn't be surprised if those two ended up getting married," Zach told Rhonda. "Billy really likes your sister."

Oscar sighed. "Alas...another lost love."

Rhonda patted Oscar on his shoulder. "Stand guard with Zach, okay? I have work to do." And with those words, she walked back to the holding cell Thorn was being held in and prepared to outsmart a killer she had given far too much credit to. No matter what, a seventeen-year-old was just that: seventeen years old. "Hello, Thorn."

Thorn leaned up from the cot he was lying on. "What do you want?"

Rhonda grinned. It was time to have a little fun. "I've come to gloat." She beamed and began teasing Thorn about being locked behind bars. "Get used to it, boy," she mocked Thorn. Thorn's face erupted with rage. Rhonda continued to grin.

"You're a dead woman!" Thorn screamed.

"Perfect," Rhonda whispered as the hidden tape recorder in her coat pocket recorded every threat Thorn threw at her.

chapter eight

"You killed Paula Capperson, and just like I promised, you're going to spend the rest of your life behind bars," Rhonda told Thorn.

"Yeah, lady, I killed that old bat, but I'm going to walk free!" Thorn yelled. He kicked the jail bars as hard as he could. "I'm going to kill Haley Wellington and then I'm coming for you!"

Rhonda grinned. "Oh really?" she asked and tapped the jail bars blocking Thorn from escaping. "And just how are you going to do that?" she asked.

"The same way I killed Old Lady Capperson...I'm going to strangle you to death," Thorn promised, allowing his youth to destroy his entire future. "Capperson tried to run, but I caught her and strangled her to death. I was going to strangle her in the snow and hide her body, but she tried to run. I would have dragged her body out into the snow after I killed her, but I was afraid someone might see. My original plan was to make her take a walk with me." Thorn narrowed his eyes. "You're going to take a walk with me, lady," he promised.

Rhonda saw a vicious killer—one far too old to be living

in the eyes of a seventeen-year-old kid—appear. The sight of the killer caused chills to run down her spine. "Why did Haley Wellington start blackmailing you for money?" she asked Thorn, throwing cold water in his face.

Thorn kicked the jail bars again. "How did you find out?" he demanded.

"I have the missing journal, genius," Rhonda snapped. "Now tell me why Haley Wellington blackmailed you."

"That girl...was meant to be fun," Thorn growled. "You know...someone to sneak off to a movie with or take a walk with...nothing serious. Just some girl to mess with on the weekends. The academy can be a boring, dry nightmare. A person can go insane up there."

"I heard you weren't allowed to date a local girl," Rhonda pointed out. "Seems to me you enjoy breaking the rules." Rhonda folded her arms. "You're engaged to a very important girl."

Thorn pointed a vicious finger at Rhonda. "You run your mouth too much, lady!"

"Why did Haley Wellington blackmail you? Did she find out you were set to marry the daughter of a high-ranking official connected to the European Union? Or maybe Haley Wellington was simply playing you for money?"

"Oh, you're dead," Thorn promised Rhonda. "Lady, if I don't kill you, someone else will. You're messing with the wrong group of people."

Rhonda shrugged. "I'm used to dealing with sewer rats, boy. Rats are rats to me. Doesn't matter if the rat is wearing rags or money signs...a rat is a rat." Rhonda locked eyes with Thorn. "Money can't buy someone self-respect, honor, and truth. A person can have all the money and power in the world and still be nothing but a rat."

Rhonda's words slapped Thorn across his face. "Money is power, lady. Power is everything. You're going to learn that."

"Boy," Rhonda said, deciding to end the conversation, "in

this life, the smartest win." Rhonda pulled the hidden tape recorder from her pocket. "Thanks for the confession. You saved me a whole lot of time and a whole lot of trouble."

Thorn stared at the tape recorder and then let out a murderous scream. "Give me that tape recorder!" he yelled and charged at the jail bars and began trying to grab at Rhonda. "Give me that recorder...now! Do you hear me! You...you're going to ruin my life!"

"Yes, I am," Rhonda promised.

"I'm going to murder you!" Thorn hollered and began kicking the jail bars. "You're dead...dead!"

Rhonda rolled her eyes and walked out of the holding area. Zach was waiting. "Sounds like you caused quite a fuss," he said.

Rhonda closed the door leading back to the holding area, cutting off Thorn's murderous threats. "I've got the confession I need," she told Zach in a proud voice. "Oscar, catch."

Oscar looked up just in time to see Rhonda throw the tape recorder at him. "What do you—"

"Change of plan, Romeo," Rhonda told Oscar. "We'll stand guard here. I need you to take that tape recorder and make as many copies of the recording as you can. Once you do that, hide the copies in different, secure locations and then bring the original back to me."

"Wow...real James Bond stuff." Oscar beamed.

"Security," Rhonda corrected Oscar in a serious voice. "Look, Romeo, you know as well as I do that Thorn Ryeberry is connected to some very powerful people. We can't risk carrying a stick into a gun fight. Now hurry."

"I will dash away like the wind, my sweet love," Oscar promised, throwing on his coat and running to the door. "I will think of thee every second we are apart," he said and threw a kiss at Rhonda.

"Just be careful," Rhonda told Oscar, actually feeling

concern for the strange little man. "Oscar, this is serious business. We're going to stick a murder charge to the son of a very powerful man. And from what you guys told me, once we do, some very bad dominoes are going to start falling." Rhonda said this even as she was unaware that Angela Ryeberry was on her way to kill her own son. "And hurry. You're needed back here."

"I am?" Oscar asked in a shocked voice.

"Look...you may be a little...odd at times, but deep down I think you're an okay guy. And right now, we need all the help we can use. So...get to your task...James Bond."

Oscar grinned from ear to ear and tore out into the snow.

"He is a strange little man, isn't he?" Zach said.

"Yeah, but...well, the little runt kinda grows on you...like a wart," Rhonda replied. "Coffee?"

"No, thanks," Zach said. He sat down on the edge of a desk and studied the door leading to the holding area. "Rhonda, you have your gun on you, right?" Rhonda patted her coat pocket. Zach nodded and began looking around the room. "I would feel better if I had a gun."

Rhonda pointed at the desk Zach was leaning against. "Bottom left-hand drawer. Look under a stack of brown folders."

Zach pulled open the drawer and did as Rhonda instructed. His hand pulled out a Rock Island Armory M206 .38 Special. "Not much, is it?"

"I prefer my Glock." Rhonda poured herself a cup of coffee. "But it's better to have something than nothing."

Zach examined the gun. "Yeah," he said, checking the barrel. "It's loaded," he told Rhonda and stuck the gun into the right pocket of his coat. Rhonda added cream and sugar to her coffee and sat down. "So we wait," Zach said.

"So we wait." Rhonda nodded. "I hope Rita and Billy find some gold nuggets. We're going to need to really pack a wallop against Thorn Ryeberry." Rhonda sipped at her coffee. "Even though I have a confession and the journal, a team of experienced lawyers can still help that kid walk free."

"Rhonda, I was a lawyer, remember?" Zach asked. "I know every trick in the book, every loophole, every technicality there is." Zach sat back down on the edge of the desk. "You questioned a minor without a lawyer present. Bad," Zach said.

"I had to act fast," Rhonda told Zach. "I know a judge would chew me alive for what I did, but I had to act before Mrs. Ryeberry arrived."

"I'm on your side," Zach promised Rhonda. "All I'm pointing out is the same thing you are: If you're going to stick a murder charge to Thorn Ryeberry, you're going to need a heavy fist to do so."

"It sickens me to the core to know that kid...that monster back there...has no remorse for his actions," Rhonda told Zach. She put down her coffee. "Paula Capperson was a human being. She didn't deserve to die. And Mayor White... all he cares about is this town. I know, Zach, I know the man means well, and Rita and I even tried to help, but..."

"But what?" Zach asked Rhonda.

Rhonda looked at Zach with tired eyes. "You wouldn't understand."

"Try me," Zach dared Rhonda. He slowly folded his arms and listened to the icy winds howling up and down the front street.

Rhonda stared at Zach, stared into a warm, intelligent, caring face—a face that was driving trucks to pay bills his ex-wife had criminally secured for him; a face that was uncertain about the future and accepting of the present. "They are all names and faces," she finally spoke. "And that's what Paula Capperson and Thorn Ryeberry will become...just names and faces in my mind."

"Okay," Zach said, "I'm all ears."

Rhonda picked her coffee back up. "Rita and I broke some serious rules to help this little town, Zach. Paula Capperson was illegally cremated. That's a big no-no, yet we looked the other way because we cared about how this town would suffer if it lost a major old nugget. For once we acted outside of the law while trying to be cops at the same time."

"Your intentions were noble."

"Yeah, maybe," Rhonda agreed, "but if Rita and I had simply done our job and arrested Thorn Ryeberry—"

"Without evidence he would have walked," Zach finished for Rhonda. He read her worried eyes. "And you both knew that, too."

"Well, Paula Capperson is ashes now. No body, no case. That's why Rita and I decided to try and make Thorn Ryeberry chase us." Rhonda sipped at her coffee. "I suppose if Paula's body would have been left alone, we might have taken a different path. Boy, we sure were thrown for a loop."

"You and Rita are only human, Rhonda. You're both taking on a great deal of responsibility for complete strangers. Me? I have to admit, I would have walked away by now and left this town to sink or swim on its own."

"I don't believe that."

Zach shrugged his shoulders. "Rhonda, I'm not a saint. When you were in the hospital in Kansas, I was more worried about getting back on the road. I didn't know you. You were a complete stranger to me. And that's how it's always been with me. I...was never good at getting close to people. Lawyers have a way of making people stand where they want them."

"Zach, why are you telling me this?" Rhonda asked in a confused voice.

Zach shrugged again. "I want to change," he confessed. "Billy took me in...pays me good money...offers me a real friendship. Why? Why should Billy care about me?"

"Billy is a good man."

"Exactly." Zach nodded. "A couple of years ago I wouldn't have given two seconds' worth of my time. My time was money." Zach looked down at the floor. "My ex-wife betrayed me...that stung. But...I'm grateful. I was brought down off my high horse and forced to see people for who they are...not how I perceive them."

"The Lord works in mysterious ways. His ways are perfect, Zach."

"I know," Zach said and looked up at Rhonda. "I'm learning what it means to be...humble in spirit. You, Rita, and Billy are teaching me."

"We are?"

"You were willing to help a town full of strangers," Zach told Rhonda. "Why? What is this town to you?"

"Well...I mean, maybe if Paula's body wouldn't have been cremated...I mean, Rita and I were still determined to catch her killer, Zach."

"Why?" Zach asked. "What was Paula Capperson to you? You sure weren't excited to make this trip to see that woman, remember?"

"Yeah, I remember."

"So why go through all this trouble?" Zach asked and then said: "I can tell you why."

"Why?"

"Because you have a heart," Zach told Rhonda and looked deeply into her beautiful face. "You, Rita, and Billy...all three of you have a heart that cares about people I always looked down on." Zach pointed to the holding area. "You've caught your killer and now you're fighting tooth and nail to ensure he gets stuck with a murder charge. You could have walked away."

"Cops never walk away."

"You're not a cop anymore, remember? You're retired," Zach reminded Rhonda.

"I…I'll always be a cop."

"Exactly." Zach leaned up and walked over to the coffee station. "You'll always care about people, Rhonda. And…that makes you very special in my eyes."

Rhonda didn't know how to respond. Zach had thrown a lot at her in a matter of minutes. She needed time to process his words. So she did what any woman on the spot would do: "Coffee?"

"I think I'm ready for a cup now." Zach slowly poured himself a cup of coffee. "So, what's the plan?" he asked, grabbing hold of a new topic.

"Wait for Rita and Billy to get back…wait for Mrs. Ryeberry to arrive…wait and see how this case plays out." Rhonda glanced down at the phone resting on the desk she was sitting at. "In the meantime, I need to make a call." Rhonda picked up the phone and called Jackson Wellington's cell phone. The conversation she had just shared with Zach felt splintered in her mind. She had tried to confess a deep emotion to him and in return he confessed a deep emotion to her; yet both sides were still foggy. Why did life have to be so…so…to say it simply: complicated? "Yes, hello, Mr. Wellington? Yes, this is Rhonda Knight…fine. Mr. Wellington, new developments in the case have surfaced and I'm afraid that your daughter still may not be out of harm's way."

Zach listened to Rhonda change from a woman who was shooting baskets with one eye open into a professional cop. He took a sip of coffee, walked to the front door, peeked outside, and then focused back on Rhonda and waited. "Haley is still unconscious? I'm sorry to hear that, Mr. Wellington." Rhonda closed her eyes and saw Haley's tender face. "Mr. Wellington, as of now, I can't make any official calls because I do not have the authority. However, I do wish to warn you to remain at your daughter's side at all times. Sheriff O'Neil… he's up at Green Valley Academy…yes…please call him.

Okay, thank you. Haley is in my prayers." Rhonda ended the call and looked up at Zach. "Okay," she said, "I did what was needed. Now we wait for the sky to grow darker and see what kind of storm we're going to be thrown into."

Zach watched Rhonda pick up her coffee and take a sip. He wanted to speak words of encouragement but instead didn't speak at all. Something deep in his gut was troubling him. He glanced toward the holding area again and felt something sinister begin chewing at his stomach.

Angela Ryeberry wasn't what Rhonda expected. Rhonda had expected an older woman wearing hateful money signs to come barging into the sheriff's office at full steam. Instead, a very beautiful, dazzling woman in her mid- to late thirties politely walked through the front door holding a worried expression. "My son, Thorn Ryeberry, is supposed to be here," she told Rhonda.

Rhonda studied Angela with careful eyes as she slowly stood up. Angela quickly brushed snow off a leather jacket that was far too thin for the weather. The woman was dressed like a sleek model rather than a mother. Snow clung to her long, silky, red hair that shined like fire. Deep, breathtaking blue eyes glowed with a beauty that even Zach found hard to resist. "Yes, your son is here," Rhonda explained. "You must be Angela Ryeberry?"

"Yes," Angela told Rhonda, keeping her voice worried. She slowly walked to the desk Rhonda was standing at and set down a small black purse. "Are you in charge?"

"For now," Rhonda explained in a calm voice. "Sheriff O'Neil is at Green Valley Academy."

Angela nodded. As she did, her eyes absorbed every feature of Rhonda. The woman was very lovely, if not simply beautiful; and dangerously smart. "I would like to see my son."

"Of course," Rhonda said, maintaining a polite police tone. "But first I need to check your purse and pat you down. I know that may be uncomfortable, but it's the rules."

Angela glanced at Zach. Zach looked down at the floor. "I understand," she said and allowed Rhonda to check the contents of her purse. Rhonda found a wallet holding a simple identification card, a passport, some credit cards, and a pack of mints. She did not find a cell phone or a weapon.

"Please raise your arms," Rhonda asked Angela in an easy voice. Angela raised her arms into the air. Rhonda carefully patted her down. She found the leather jacket's pockets empty and didn't feel any hidden items. Then her hands reached a pair of ankle-high black boots. "Mrs. Ryeberry, I'm afraid I..." Rhonda hesitated.

"My boots. Of course." Angela politely removed her boots. "Okay?" Rhonda nodded, satisfied that Angela seemed clear. "May I see my son now?"

"Yes."

Angela put her boots back on and grabbed her purse. "May I take my purse?"

"Sure," Rhonda said. "Zach, will you watch the front?" Zach nodded. "This way, Mrs. Ryeberry."

Angela followed Rhonda to the holding area. When she saw her son lying on a cot, her heart grew very angry and very bitter; not toward Rhonda or even her own husband, but toward her son. "May we be alone?"

Rhonda studied Thorn. Thorn shot her a vicious eye. "Mrs. Ryeberry, I know this may be very difficult for you to hear, but your son murdered an innocent woman. Now, I understand you're a very powerful woman and I don't doubt that you're going to try to protect your son. But please know I'm not the enemy. I'm simply doing my duty as a cop. I wish...it could be different."

Angela saw a tenderness in Rhonda that she respected. Of course, Rhonda was simply doing her job. Good people all over the world were doing their jobs. That's why she was fighting her husband—fighting evil. Of course, she was no saint. Angela Ryeberry had made many errors in her past and wasn't about to stop. But her mission was to change Europe for the better—to help create a new political party that would govern Europe with intelligence rather than control; common sense rather than hatred. Yes, the new party would be just one step under communism, but the party would rule in favor of the people instead of against; the party would reprogram people how to think and act in order to create a new Europe that would refashion the world and create an ideal model for a one-world government controlled by "certain" elected officials. And Thorn Ryeberry, her dear son, was endangering her lifelong mission. "Hello, Thorn."

"Mother," Thorn said in a cold voice.

Angela looked at Rhonda. "You are not my enemy," she promised. "If my son is guilty of the crime you mentioned, he will answer to justice. His father and I fully understand the temper that sleeps in his heart. We have always been very concerned."

"I'll leave you alone. Call me when you're ready to leave." Rhonda left Angela alone with Thorn, walked back to Zach, and waited.

"You fool," Angela snapped at Thorn. "You have endangered everything."

"Me?" Thorn snapped back. He jumped to his feet. "You're the one who insisted on getting Old Lady Capperson fired. You're the one who told Tulley to watch my every move."

"We sent you to this country to receive education." Angela stared at Thorn with sour eyes. "You have caused a great deal of trouble by breaking the rules."

"Me?" Thorn complained like a pouty child. "You were the one who insisted Capperson get fired."

"Because she saw you in town with Haley Wellington, you..." Angela bit down on her tongue. "Ms. Capperson reported your violation to Mr. Tulley. Mr. Tulley contacted me. That is when I knew Ms. Capperson had to be fired. And, yes, that is when I ordered Mr. Tulley to begin tracking your actions."

"I was just having a little fun."

"You are due to marry the daughter of our enemy," Angela snapped at her son. "You know as well as anyone, Thorn, how delicate our situation is. If Brian Mertington finds out you were dating a local girl, he will cancel the engagement. Brian Mertington will not tolerate disobedience."

"Brian Mertington is a moron," Thorn complained. "I didn't want to get married to his stuffy daughter anyway."

Angela shook her head. "Thorn, you were supposed to play by the rules."

"Your rules," Thorn continued to complain. "But don't worry, Mother, I covered your tracks. I killed Capperson and I'll make sure Haley Wellington will end up six feet under and then I'll go after that stupid cop." Thorn was about to tell Angela that Rhonda had recorded his confession and that Haley had been blackmailing him, but he bit down on his tongue. It was better to keep things simple instead of further infuriating his mother.

"I'm your adopted mother." Angela narrowed her eyes. "Yet I have always considered you as my real son. I have loved you as my real son, Thorn...sheltered you, nurtured you...protected you. And how have you repaid me?"

"Look, Mother," Thorn growled, "just get me out of here, okay? I have work to do and then we can fly back to Europe."

"No," she informed Thorn. "Your....my husband has given me a choice: you or me."

"What?" Thorn gasped.

"My husband has discovered my secret meetings, Thorn," Angela explained. She slowly lifted her left boot and removed the heel. "I'm sorry, Thorn. I trusted you with all of my deepest secrets. You failed me. Now you must die," she said in a sad voice.

Thorn's eyes grew wide as he watched Angela remove a small bag full of a tan-colored powder. "Hey, what is that?" he asked. Angela carefully opened the bag, poured the powder into her hands, and then, without any warning, blew the powder into Thorn's face. Thorn grabbed his face, stumbled backward, and began coughing. Seconds later, he dropped down onto the floor and stopped moving. Angela quickly replaced the bag in the heel of her boot and waited five minutes for the powder on Thorn's face to evaporate. Once the powder evaporated, she called out to Rhonda in a panicked voice.

Rhonda ran into the holding area, spotted Thorn lying on his back, and threw her eyes at Angela. "What happened?" she demanded.

"He...collapsed," Angela explained in a shaky voice. "Please, call an ambulance. Hurry."

Rhonda wasn't sure if she was being set up. She studied Thorn. The boy appeared unconscious, but she wasn't about to fall for any tricks. "Zach!" Zach ran into the holding area. "Cover me. You stand back," she told Angela. Angela stepped back away from the holding cell as Zach yanked out his gun.

"Ready," Zach told Rhonda.

Rhonda nodded, removed her own gun, unlocked the holding cell, and carefully stepped inside. She moved toward Thorn's unconscious body, kicked his leg, and then looked over her shoulder at Angela. Angela had her hands clasped together. "Okay," she whispered and cautiously bent down and checked Thorn for a pulse. "No pulse...he's not breathing. Go call an ambulance!" she called out to Zach. Zach raced off.

"My son," Angela said and began to allow a few fake tears to leave her eyes.

Rhonda studied Zach's face. As far as she could see, the deadly young man showed no signs of being violently attacked. As a matter of fact, his face appeared as if he had simply fallen asleep. "Any idea what happened?"

"We were talking and he suddenly collapsed," Angela cried. "Please, do something for my son."

Rhonda felt for a pulse again and shook her head. "I can't find a pulse, Mrs. Ryeberry," she said in a sorrowful voice and stood up. "I'm afraid your son is dead."

"Can't you start CPR?" Angela begged.

Rhonda shook her head no. Thorn Ryeberry was dead. No amount of CPR was going to save him. The only question Rhonda had was how Angela Ryeberry had killed her son. She had checked the woman from top to bottom. "Mrs. Ryeberry, I've seen many dead bodies in my time. Your son is dead."

Angela began to lift her hands to her mouth but stopped. Instead, she rushed out of the holding area. Rhonda quickly followed. "Oh, this is so horrible," Angela cried. "I need...to be alone. Is there a bathroom?"

"There." Rhonda pointed to a door leading into a public bathroom. Angela nodded, raced into the bathroom, and immediately washed her hands. "The boy is dead," Rhonda told Zach in a confused voice.

Zach put down the telephone he was holding. "Ambulance is on the way," he informed Rhonda and then looked toward the holding area. "Any ideas?"

Rhonda tossed a thumb toward the bathroom door. "Her," she whispered. "It's the only explanation."

Zach nodded. "Thorn was a healthy boy. What other explanation can there be?" he whispered back.

"Watch our friend," Rhonda told Zach. She walked back to the holding area, entered Thorn's cell, and began to examine his body. "Your face smells like...I can't place it," she said in a frustrated voice. "How did she kill you, Thorn?" Rhonda stared into the boy's dead face. She felt relief that a deadly monster was dead...yet, as she stared into Thorn's face, she saw a sleeping seventeen-year-old kid who had died far too young. Torn between her emotions, sobered by the reality of death once more, Rhonda stood up. "Why couldn't you have just been a normal kid, huh?" she asked and then walked back to Zach. Angela was sitting at a desk. "Mrs. Ryeberry, I'm very sorry."

Angela wiped at her tears. "Yes, so am I."

"If you'll excuse me," Rhonda said and pointed at the bathroom. "I need to clear my mind."

"Of course." Angela nodded.

Rhonda thanked Angela and walked into the bathroom. The bathroom was small, clean, and smelled of pine wood. Rhonda was interested in the design of the bathroom. She hurried to a small metal trash can and fished out a damp paper towel Angela had used to dry her hands with. "Let's see," Rhonda whispered and very carefully took a sniff of the paper towel. "The same smell that is on Thorn Ryeberry's face." Rhonda shoved the paper towel into her coat pocket, washed her hands, and left the bathroom. As she did, she heard ambulance sirens in the distance. "Mrs. Ryeberry, I will need you to stay behind and write out a statement. I know this is a very difficult time, but I have rules to follow."

"I understand," Angela told Rhonda as the ambulance sirens grew closer and closer. "I must call my husband. Is there a private room I can use?"

Before Rhonda could answer, Mayor White burst through the front door. "Oh, Mrs. Ryeberry, I just heard. I'm so very sorry," he said, rushing to Angela and taking her hands.

"Please accept my deepest sympathies." Mayor White threw a hard eye at Rhonda.

"Thank you, Mayor White," Angela said as tears left her eyes. "But this situation is nobody's fault except...my son's. My son chose to kill an innocent woman and now he is dead. I expect his heart gave out. My son had a heart condition. I fear the excitement was too much for him."

Rhonda watched Mayor White sit Angela down. "Now, now," he said in a soothing voice, "everything is going to be all right, Mrs. Ryeberry."

"My son was not well, I'm afraid," Angela spoke through her tears. "My husband and I both were aware that he had a mental condition as well as a health condition. We had hoped the serenity of the Vermont countryside would be healthy for both of his conditions. Oh, I'm so sorry for all the trouble."

"Not at all...not at all," Mayor White continued to soothe Angela.

"We'll be outside, Mrs. Ryeberry," Rhonda said in a polite voice. She nodded at Zach. Zach followed Rhonda out into the snow. "I don't know how she sneaked the murder weapon past me," she whispered as the racing ambulance approached, throwing blaring lights into the snow, "but I know she used some form of poison."

"Poison?" Zach asked. "Rhonda, Thorn Ryeberry didn't strike me as the type of kid who would stand around and willingly be poisoned." Zach focused on the approaching ambulance. "She couldn't have entered the holding cell...so how?"

"Exactly," Rhonda said. "And even worse...what do we do now? Thorn Ryeberry is dead...what does it matter if we have his confession...the journal?" Rhonda sighed. "It wouldn't matter if Rita and Billy located the lost emails. This case is...over." Rhonda watched the ambulance screech to a stop in front of the sheriff's office. "The killer has been killed...and there's no way I can prove that Mrs. Ryeberry performed the act." Rhonda let her shoulders fall. "I need to call Rita."

Zach watched Rhonda walk down the snowy sidewalk in order to get out of the way of two paramedics. He threw his hands into the pockets of his coat and looked around at the falling snow. It sure seemed like the case was over. But deep down he wondered…was it really over? Zach didn't know. What he did know was that, like her son, Angela Ryeberry was a killer.

chapter nine

R ita looked up at Billy with excited eyes. "Bingo," she said.

Billy had no idea what Rita was doing on the funny-looking laptop sitting on a fancy desk. He rubbed the back of his neck, glanced around a gloomy writing room that smelled of flowers and looked like the inside of a wooden rose, and shrugged his shoulders. "If you say we struck gold, I reckon I'll take your word for it."

Rita checked a gray printer that was connected to the laptop. "Billy, the numbers were a password," she explained in a quick voice. "I was able to log in to Paula's laptop and locate a file holding all the emails Paula had stolen from Thorn Ryeberry. And look..." Rita pointed at the computer screen. "This file shows that Paula rented a safety deposit box at the bank. My guess is she put all the hard copies of the emails into the safety deposit box. I could be wrong."

"Wrong ain't wrong until you tangle with the answer," Billy told Rita.

Rita gave Billy a loving smile. "Right," she agreed and began printing off all the emails. As soon as the first email began to print, her cell phone rang. "That must be Rhonda." Rita quickly answered the call. "Great news—"

"Bad news," Rhonda said, standing out in the cold snow. "Angela Ryeberry arrived, Rita. She managed to kill Thorn Ryeberry with some kind of poison. There's no way to prove that, though. Zach and I were standing in the front office when she killed her own son. This case is...over." Rhonda watched the paramedics rush into the sheriff's office. "I'm ready to go home, Sis. Let this town...let Mayor White...sift through this mess."

Rita looked up at Billy with upset eyes. "Thorn Ryeberry is dead. Rhonda said Angela Ryeberry, his mother, killed him with some type of poison."

"Now isn't that something evil for a momma to do?" Billy asked in a disgusted voice. "Why...that woman ought to be took out and strung up. Don't matter if her boy was no good...ain't for her to do such a thing. Bible says there's supposed to be two or more witnesses against a person before he's proclaimed guilty. Last time I checked that boy had no witnesses against him...he just ran his mouth to your sister in a mighty stupid way. Now I ain't defending him, no sir, but still...for a momma to do such a thing...why, it's sickening, that's what it is...plum sickening to the core."

"Yes, Billy, it is. Murder in itself is sickening to the core." Rita watched the emails continue to print. "I was able to access Paula's laptop, Rhonda. I located the emails and a file showing Paula rented a safety deposit box at the local bank."

Rhonda wiped snow away from her face. "A safety deposit box?" she asked.

"Yes."

A thought slipped into Rhonda's mind. "Rita, Jackson Wellington runs the bank," she said. "I wonder if... somehow...Haley Wellington?" Rhonda looked down at the snowy sidewalk she was standing on. "Or maybe Jackson Wellington himself?"

"You're wondering if someone stole the hard copies and used them to blackmail Thorn Ryeberry?"

"Yes," Rhonda confirmed. "And I wonder if...let's assume that Haley Wellington did somehow steal the hard copies?"

"But how?" Rita asked. "It would have to have been Jackson Wellington."

Rhonda thought for a few seconds. "You're right," she said. "Rita, could it be Jackson Wellington was forcing his daughter to blackmail Thorn Ryeberry?"

"The daughter does the dirty work while the dad keeps his hands clean. Could be?" Rita nodded. "If we're on the right track that means Jackson Wellington is still in possession of the hard copies."

"Which means he has ammunition to fight with...or get himself killed with," Rhonda worried. "I wonder if Angela Ryeberry knows the emails were stolen?" Rhonda wiped more snow away from her face. "No...if that spider had known about the emails she would have killed her son and the Wellington family long ago."

"Agreed," Rita stated.

"Which makes me wonder if Thorn Ryeberry spilled the beans," Rhonda said. "I...I don't think he did. I mean, the kid was already in enough hot water...surely he didn't want to make his mother even madder?"

Rita saw Billy staring down at the emails that were printing. "Billy?" she asked.

"Just plum sickening," Billy said. "Ain't right for a momma to do such a thing. Reckon we need to think about switching gears and making sure that woman gets a dose of justice."

"I'm not sure how, Billy," Rita confessed. "Angela Ryeberry is a powerful woman. We have no evidence to prove she killed her son."

"I did manage to get Thorn to confess to killing Paula," Rhonda told Rita. "I have Oscar making recordings of the confession right now. And we do have the journal...and the emails. If we're smart, maybe we can trick Angela

Ryeberry…" Rhonda sighed. "No…enough is enough," she said. "The more we tried to help in this case, the worse it got. A cop has to know when to back down, Sis. It's time to go home."

Rita felt anger touch her cheeks. "I don't want to give up."

"What can we do?" Rhonda asked. "We've made a mess of things."

"No, we haven't," Rita insisted.

"Sis, all of our plans backfired," Rhonda pointed out. "Even when we stopped playing nice and threw justice at Thorn Ryeberry, our plan backfired. The kid is dead and there's nothing we can do about it." Rhonda shook her head. "If we try to tangle with Angela Ryeberry, we'll make ourselves a bad enemy. Is it worth it?" Rhonda glanced toward the ambulance. "Sis, the kid who murdered Paula is dead. Justice has been served. Let's not push it and end up with two bodies lying in the back of an ambulance."

Rita was surprised at her sister. "Are you actually backing down?" she asked.

"Look, I'm not backing down," Rhonda told Rita in an upset voice. "I agreed to come to Vermont with you to attend a wedding I didn't even want to go to. Ever since we arrived in town it's been one twist and turn after another. First Paula confessed her silly little truths to us…and then we meet Oscar Frost…oh boy, did we. And then Paula ends up dead…Mayor White demands we don't investigate her death…he has her body cremated…and, like idiots, we decided to pursue justice while trying to prevent this little town from losing a strong source of income. Through it all, a teenage girl tried to kill herself, I had to kiss Oscar Frost, deal with a snotty headmaster who was blackmailing the mayor…and now the killer himself has been knocked off by his own mother. Rita, I'd say it's time to call it quits. We gave this case the good old college try, but enough is enough."

Rita knew Rhonda was right. She let out a heavy sigh and

studied the printing emails. "Okay, Rhonda, I suppose you are making sense."

"I am making sense," Rhonda told Rita. "I am also very hungry and cold. All I want to do is go to the café, get a good hot meal down, rest my eyes until morning, and fly back home to Clovedale Falls."

Rita watched the last email print, and then the printer went silent, throwing what felt like a funeral cloth over the entire case. "Okay, Sis," Rita promised, "we're...officially off this case. I'll erase all the data on Paula's computer, secure the emails I just printed in my purse, and meet you at the sheriff's office."

"I'll secure the journal pages and when Oscar returns, I'll make him bring me all the copies of Thorn Ryeberry's confession he made."

"Deal."

"See you in a bit." Rhonda ended the call and waited until the paramedics rolled Thorn Ryeberry's body out into the snow before walking back inside. Angela Ryeberry was standing in a corner talking with Mayor White. Zach was perched near the coffee station sipping on a cup of coffee. "I talked to Rita. We're going home," she said in a voice loud enough for Angela Ryeberry and Mayor White to hear.

Mayor White hurried over to Rhonda. "I've spoken with Mrs. Ryeberry. She is willing to overlook the illegal actions taken against her son," he told Rhonda in a stern voice. "I would suggest you leave town immediately with your sister before she changes her mind."

Rhonda looked at Angela. "I only want my son to rest in peace now," Angela spoke through teary eyes. "What is done is done. Nothing is going to bring back my son." Angela wiped at her tears. "I am going to have his body flown to France and buried in a family plot."

Rhonda was too tired to argue. "Mayor White, my sister and I are going to stay the night in Mayfield and leave first thing in the morning. We're both far too exhausted to travel right now. We're going to eat a hot meal at the café, go back to our room, and rest. We'll be out of your hair before ten o'clock tomorrow morning."

"See that you are," Mayor White ordered Rhonda, struggling to maintain a forceful voice in front of Mrs. Ryeberry. Deep down in a place that he kept hidden from the world, the man actually respected all that Rita and Rhonda had tried to accomplish. "Please," he added, "leave town."

Rhonda nodded. "Mrs. Ryeberry, I guess this is goodbye. The best of…uh, luck."

"Thank you," Angela said. "Mayor White, will you please drive me to the hospital? I must call my husband and begin making the proper arrangements."

"Of course," Mayor White said and carefully walked Angela out into the snow.

"And there goes a cold-blooded killer," Rhonda told Zach in an angry tone. "And there's absolutely nothing we can do about it."

Zach wanted to offer words of encouragement to Rhonda but couldn't think of any. "Well," he said, "what's done is done. At least a small portion of justice was served on behalf of Paula Capperson."

"Yeah, I guess," Rhonda said and simply shook her head. "I need to get the journal pages and go find Oscar. When Rita arrives, we can go eat and then rest for the night."

"I think that sounds like a good idea," Zach agreed. He put down his coffee, walked to the front door, opened it, and saw Angela Ryeberry walking across the street with Mayor White toward a gray truck. Mayor White helped Angela into the passenger seat. "A real good idea," he said and closed the door.

Angela saw Zach close the front door and slowly waited for Mayor White to drive her to the hospital. An hour later, she walked into a private bathroom and called her husband. "Thorn is dead. I'm having his body flown to France."

"Did anybody see you?" Kent Ryeberry asked. He stood up from an expensive leather chair, walked across a glossy hardwood floor, and stopped at a window.

"No."

Kent peered down at the busy streets of London. "Very good," he said. "Return home and stop playing games. I can't protect your life if you insist on being foolish. I have pardoned you this time, but you won't get a second chance."

"I understand," Angela told Kent.

Kent loved his wife but knew her end had come. Angela Ryeberry's death had been ordered. "Return home, Angela, and stop being foolish."

"I will fly back first thing tomorrow. I am far too exhausted to travel at this moment, Kent."

"Very well," Kent said. "I will expect you back in London no later than tomorrow evening." He ended the call. "Goodbye, Angela," he said to himself. "I'm sorry it had to be this way." Kent slowly dialed a number. "She is not to leave Vermont alive."

"Yes, Mr. Ryeberry," a deadly voice said, standing outside of the hospital.

"The information you retrieved from Oscar Frost was most helpful. When you finish with Angela, return to London and receive your payment." Kent looked down at the busy streets below. "I'm going to need to locate a new wife," he whispered and forced his mind to completely forget about Angela.

Angela, unaware that her death had been ordered, washed her face and stepped out of the bathroom. To her surprise, she saw Rhonda waiting for her. "Ms. Knight...what are you doing here?"

"Being very stupid," Rhonda said. She yanked out a pair of handcuffs and tried to handcuff Angela. Angela quickly slapped Rhonda's hands away. "Don't resist," Rhonda warned.

"How dare you!" Angela snapped. "Where is Mayor White? I demand to see him."

Rita stepped up behind Angela. "Mrs. Ryeberry, this is for your own protection," she explained.

"Yes," Rhonda confirmed in a quick voice. "Don't ask any questions."

Angela stared into Rhonda's eyes. "What is this about?"

Oscar appeared with Billy and Zach. The poor man's face looked as if it had been sent through a meat grinder. "That," Rhonda explained.

Angela froze. "What happened to that man?"

"I got beat up...duh." Oscar grabbed his jaw. "Oh...it hurts to talk."

"I sent Oscar to make copies of the murder confession your son made," Rhonda told Angela. "A man wearing a black suit followed Oscar to his apartment—"

"And beat the snot out of me," Oscar told Angela. "I kinda...well...I confessed everything..."

"Everything?" Angela asked. "What is this 'everything'?" she demanded.

Rhonda glanced around. The hallway was secure. "The man who hurt Oscar will most likely try to kill you," she stated in a firm tone.

"I don't—"

"Look, sister," Rhonda snapped, "I know you killed your son. I smelled the poison on his face and smelled the same poison you wiped on the paper towel when you went into the bathroom back at the sheriff's office."

Angela looked around at the faces staring at her. Billy's face was especially unpleasant. "Leave me alone...this instant," she demanded.

"If we do, you're dead," Rhonda told Angela. "Now, that would be just fine with me because I'm sick of this case. It's been nothing but a three-ring circus the entire time. But, unfortunately, I'm still a cop, lady, and I can't let someone stick a knife in your back."

"You have no idea who you're dealing with," Angela snapped at Rhonda. "If my husband has ordered my death... then I'm a dead woman no matter what. You can't help me. Now leave me alone."

"I can help," Rhonda promised. "I don't want to...but I can."

"You killed your boy, lady," Billy said in a disgusted voice, "we shouldn't even be caring what happens to the likes of you. But see, these two ladies have a goodness in their hearts that won't let them let the fella we spotted outside kill you."

Angela looked into Rhonda's eyes and then focused on Rita. Justice had certainly come back to haunt her.

"I saw them walk your wife out in handcuffs, Mr. Kent. Your wife was screaming that she didn't kill your son. What should I do?" a man wearing a black trench coat asked Kent Ryeberry.

"Where are you?"

"Watching the sheriff's office," the man explained.

Kent gritted his teeth. Before he could respond, he saw an incoming call from Angela. "I'll call you back," he snapped and answered Angela's call. "Where are you?"

"Alive," Angela told Kent. "Your hired killer hasn't harmed me...yet." Angela held up a copy of one of the emails she had sent Thorn. "I have made some friends, Kent...some friends who have very damaging information on all of your...acquaintances."

"What are you talking about?" Kent demanded.

"I sent Thorn emails with certain information pertaining to certain people you do business with," Angela explained. "I also sent him files from your computer that I stole. Thorn and I were planning to use the information against you and your fellow partners. Unfortunately, those emails have fallen into the hands of my new friends. It seems that Ms. Capperson, the woman you were concerned over and had me try to terminate, managed to access Thorn's emails."

Kent gritted his teeth. "You're lying."

"Very well," Angela said and read the email she was holding to Kent. She read off the names of four powerful men who could have Kent killed in a matter of seconds. Then she named off stolen security codes. "Shall I continue?" Angela asked.

Kent began to sweat. "You...I...how?" he demanded. "I had you watched every second of every day."

"Yes, you had me watched, but not the people working for me," Angela explained.

"What a story." Oscar beamed and then winced in pain. "This is going to be some book! We have everything... murder...romance...foreign enemies...twists and turns....and snow to boot. Ow." Oscar grabbed his jaw.

"Stop talking," Rhonda whispered.

Angela shook her head at Oscar. "Kent, call off your hired killer or this information goes public. If you call off your killer, I'll vanish into thin air. I have plenty of money stored in private accounts. You'll never hear from me again."

"You must die, or I die," Kent told Angela. "Your death has already been ordered."

"Then order your man to lie," Angela fired back. "Order him to say he killed me and then call him off."

Kent wiped sweat from his face. He was between a rock and hard place. "All right...very well. I'll do as you asked. But if you ever show your face again, Angela—"

"I won't," Angela promised. "You...just make sure Thorn's body is buried."

"Very well." Kent closed his eyes. "Goodbye, Angela," he

said and quickly called his hired killer. "I'll pay you triple to do what I say."

"Yes, sir," the deadly killer agreed and listened to Kent talk. When Kent finished, the killer simply walked away into the snow and let Angela live.

Angela looked at Rita and Rhonda. "Now what?" she asked in an uncertain voice. "You're not going to just let me walk away. I did kill my son...my adopted son."

"Don't make no matter if he was adopted," Billy told Angela. "You did a rotten thing."

Rita looked at Rhonda. "Well?"

Rhonda looked into Angela's eyes. "Take those emails... those journal pages... all of it, and take a hike, sister."

Angela stared at Rhonda in shock. "You're going to let me walk out of here?"

"What choice do we have?" Rhonda asked. "If we send you to prison, your husband will surely have you killed. We can't do that, not with a clear conscience anyway." Rhonda handed Angela the journal pages. "Paula Capperson's murderer is dead, and that's enough for us."

"Just remember what we did for you today," Rita warned Angela.

"You saved my life," Angela responded in a grateful voice. "I won't forget."

"Get out of here," Billy told Angela. "You ain't no saint, lady."

"No, I'm not a saint," Angela agreed. "Mr. Northfield, I'm a woman with a purpose...a purpose you will never understand. My battlefield is the mind. I battle ideas and words that can change the world. And, unfortunately, as with every battle, there are casualties." Angela looked toward the back hallway. "Thank you for sparing my life," she said and hurried away without saying another word.

"Ah, get out of here," Billy said and threw his hands at Angela. "Good riddance to you."

Rhonda plopped down in a desk chair. "Well, there she goes," she told Rita. "We just let a killer walk free."

Rita leaned against a desk. "What choice did we have, Rhonda? I know our decision wasn't practical...but wasn't our purpose to avenge Paula's death? I think that woman did the job for us. Besides, letting her run free...she'll be running for the rest of her life. And that, Sis, is real punishment. That woman will never have another decent night's sleep in her life...she'll always be looking over her shoulder... wondering...running...scared."

"Oh, this is good stuff," Oscar exclaimed and grabbed his cheek again.

"Little fella, you ain't got no sense, do you?" Billy fussed. He shook his head and put his arm around Oscar. "I reckon you better come back to Georgia with me for a bit. You're going to need some tending to."

"What?" Rhonda exclaimed. "Billy, wait just a second... you can't be serious?"

"Why, sure I am," Billy stated in a stubborn voice. "This little fella needs some tending to and I'm going to be the one to do the tending. Besides, I have a spare room he can sleep in."

Oscar beamed. "Oh, my sweet loves...parting isn't going to be such sweet sorrow after all."

Rita and Rhonda both moaned. "Oh no."

Zach grinned. "Well, I don't know about you, but I'm starved."

Oscar touched his cheek. "I...think I'll get a milkshake."

Billy smiled. "Come on then," he said and then suddenly stopped. "Uh-oh!"

"What?" Rita asked in an alarmed voice. "Billy, what's the matter?"

"Chester," Billy said and made a pained face. "I was supposed to call him today and say howdy. I promised. Oh, he's gonna be cranky for sure!" Billy pulled out his cell phone and called the dog hotel Chester was staying in. "Yeah...this is Billy Northfield...Chester Northfield is staying with you folks...I need to say howdy to him and fast." Billy looked around and waited on anxious legs. A few minutes later, a sweet voice told Billy that he was holding the phone to Chester's ear. "Hey, Chester old buddy, how are you? I know I'm late calling you, but...well, it's been busy." The girl holding the phone to Chester's ear told Billy the dog was flapping his left ear. "Oh...Chester, don't be mad...I...got sidetracked is all." Chester wasn't in the mood for excuses. He tucked his head away from the phone and began plotting how to get even with Billy. Billy slowly put his cell phone away and winced. "I'm in some hot water, yes sir."

Rita grinned. "Come on, Billy, let's go eat and—"

Mayor White burst through the front door. "Where is she?" he demanded. "How dare you arrest Mrs. Ryeberry... you...you...sour cherries!"

"Twin cherries is more fitting." Rhonda grinned. "Mayor White, everything is fine."

"How is everything fine?" Mayor White asked in a frantic voice. "Parents are flying in from all over the world and yanking their children out of the academy!"

"So what's the big deal about a few snotty kids being taken out of school?" Billy asked. "Listen, fella, Rita told me all about that there academy and all the good land it sits on. If you had any sense you would turn that land into a nice farm, plant yourselves some apple trees, run some cornfields... shoot, there's all kinds of potential. Why, even if you weren't interested in farming you could turn the building into a small college...and even have other buildings added. Shoot, you act like the end of the world has come. You just ain't thinking straight is all."

"College?" Mayor White repeated. "I never considered that."

"A private Christian college would be nice," Rita told

Mayor White. "You have the land. All you have to do is promote the idea and I'm sure someone will bite. And," she added, "if someone does bite, separate buildings will need to be built...libraries...study halls...classrooms...dorms."

"Employment, employment, employment," Rhonda added. "More people can be employed by a functional college than a private academy, Mayor White."

Mayor White rubbed his chin. "Why, that is a great idea," he said, calming down. "Why, I have many friends who could assist me in attracting potential customers. Yes...a college...." Mayor White actually smiled. "We'll need to construct more buildings...." Mayor White slowly walked back out into the snow.

Rhonda rolled her eyes. "And I thought Clovedale Falls was special."

"Let's go eat," Rita laughed, "and get out of town before someone else drops dead."

Three days later, Rita and Rhonda walked into their small bakery on sore legs. Oscar hurried in behind them and shook cold rain off a red rain jacket. "Say, this is nice," he said. "My two loves really know how to live the good life."

Rhonda tossed a white purse down onto the front counter and then rubbed her legs. "I can't believe we're home," she moaned.

"I know," Rita moaned back. "I can't believe Chester is still mad at Billy." Rita removed her coat and brushed at her dark blue dress. "Thanks for spilling coffee on me, Oscar."

"Anytime, my love." Oscar beamed.

Rhonda slapped her forehead, took off her coat, and pointed at her brown dress. It was covered with white powder. "He got me with a donut."

"Love marks," Oscar promised and winked at Rhonda.

"Oh, don't make me bake you into a muffin," Rhonda warned Oscar.

Billy and Zach walked through the front door of the bakery before Rhonda could threaten Oscar further. "Well," Billy said, fighting back a yawn, "I think I'm going to take the little fella out to the farm and get some shut-eye. Sure was nice of you girls to drive with Chester instead of flying."

"We had no choice, Billy. Chester refused to ride with you," Rita told Billy.

Zach looked out at the front street and saw Chester sitting in Billy's truck. "He's still pretty upset."

"Yep," Billy nodded, "that dog is going to be one mad hornet for a while. But so what? He'll get over acting childish." Billy looked at Rita. Rita sure was pretty. "I'll come into town and see you tomorrow."

"We'll be here," Rita promised. She smiled at Billy with loving eyes. "Thanks, Billy...for being so great."

"Me? Great? Ah, get out of here." Billy threw his arm around Oscar. "Let's go, little fella."

"Until tomorrow, my loves," Oscar called out and left the bakery with Billy.

Zach looked at Rhonda. He wanted to say something, but it was clear the lovely woman was exhausted. "I'll see you, okay?"

Rhonda walked over to Zach and kissed his cheek. "Come into town with Billy tomorrow."

"Really?" Zach asked in a surprised voice.

Rhonda nodded. "We'll let our friendship see where it leads." She smiled.

Zach stumbled back toward the front door, bumped into a shelf holding candy bars, blushed, and hurried outside into the cold rain.

"He likes you." Rita smiled.

"Yeah, I can kinda tell that," Rhonda sighed. She watched Zach help Oscar into the front of Billy's truck and then laughed when Chester crawled away from Billy and plopped down in Zach's lap. Billy threw his hands into the air and fussed at nothing. "It's good to be home."

Rita watched Billy drive away and then walked into the back kitchen and began making a pot of coffee. "Remind me to never attend another wedding ever again," she said.

Rhonda hopped up onto the kitchen counter. "You know, in the movies and in books, everything is nice and orderly. The good guy wears nice suits and always catches the bad guy. Boy, I sure wish it was like that in real life."

Rita nodded. "I don't think I'm ever going to see Vermont the same way."

Rhonda watched Rita get the coffee going. Soon a fresh, delicious scent filled the damp kitchen air. "Maybe we can visit Alaska next," she teased. "We can travel to Alaska and try to figure out who killed a polar bear. Or, better yet, we can travel into the desert and try to track down the person who kicked over a cactus."

"How about we stay home and focus on our bakery," Rita suggested. "The Pumpkin Festival may be over, but we have our bakery to run." Rita looked around the kitchen. "Now that the tourists have all left, we have to focus on the locals."

"Yeah, I suppose." Rhonda nodded and let out a tired laugh. As she did, Erma walked into the kitchen holding a yellow umbrella. "Oh...Erma, you startled us."

Erma smiled. "How was your trip?" she asked. She removed her gray raincoat, hung it up, and tossed a blue apron over her pretty yellow dress. "I want all the details while we whip up a fresh batch of muffins and get the bakery ready to open."

"Details?" Rhonda gulped.

"Details?" Rita moaned.

"All the details." Erma smiled as she took a bag of flour down from a kitchen cabinet. "Off the counter, sweetie," she told Rhonda and patted Rhonda's leg.

Rhonda slid down off the counter. "Uh...Erma, I just remembered...I have a chore to run. Rita will tell you all about our trip...she'll give you all the details you want."

"Hey...wait—"

Rhonda ran to the kitchen door and spun around. "You're the one who made me go to Vermont with you, Sis," she grinned. "Revenge is sweet."

Rita watched Rhonda vanish. Erma gave her a sweet smile. "Well, details," she said, beaming.

Rita gave a pained smile and then rubbed her eyes. "Well, it was like this," she told Erma and began to tell Erma about the very difficult and confusing case.

Far away, in a busy hospital in Vermont, Angela Ryeberry walked up to Haley Wellington's hospital room door with a man wearing nurse's scrubs walking beside her. "You know what to do," she said. "While you conduct your business, I'll conduct mine."

"What about the two lady cops?" the man asked. "Are you going to kill them, too?"

"No," Angela said. "I was shown mercy...I'll show mercy. Just this once." Angela walked away into the crowded hallway wearing a white lab coat. "Yes, Rita and Rhonda Knight showed me mercy," she whispered. "If only they knew how close they came to dying. Those two twin cherries are very lucky."

As Angela walked away, Rhonda grabbed her coat and hurried outside into the cold rain. She quickly walked into the candle shop next door and began browsing...just grateful to be home and out of sight of a crazy, insane world. What she didn't know was that the crazy world she was now hiding from was about to peek its head into Clovedale Falls and say hello once again.

more from wendy

about wendy meadows

Wendy Meadows is a USA Today bestselling author whose stories showcase women sleuths. To date, she has published dozens of books, which include her popular Sweetfern Harbor series, Sweet Peach Bakery series, and Alaska Cozy series, to name a few. She lives in the "Granite State" with her husband, two sons, two mini pigs and a lovable Labradoodle.

Join Wendy's newsletter to stay up-to-date with new releases. As a subscriber, you'll also get BLACKVINE MANOR, the complete series, for FREE!

Join Wendy's Newsletter Here
wendymeadows.com/cozy